WORSHIPERS OF THE BLACK HOLE

Thea Gregory

ISBN: 978-1-0693415-0-1

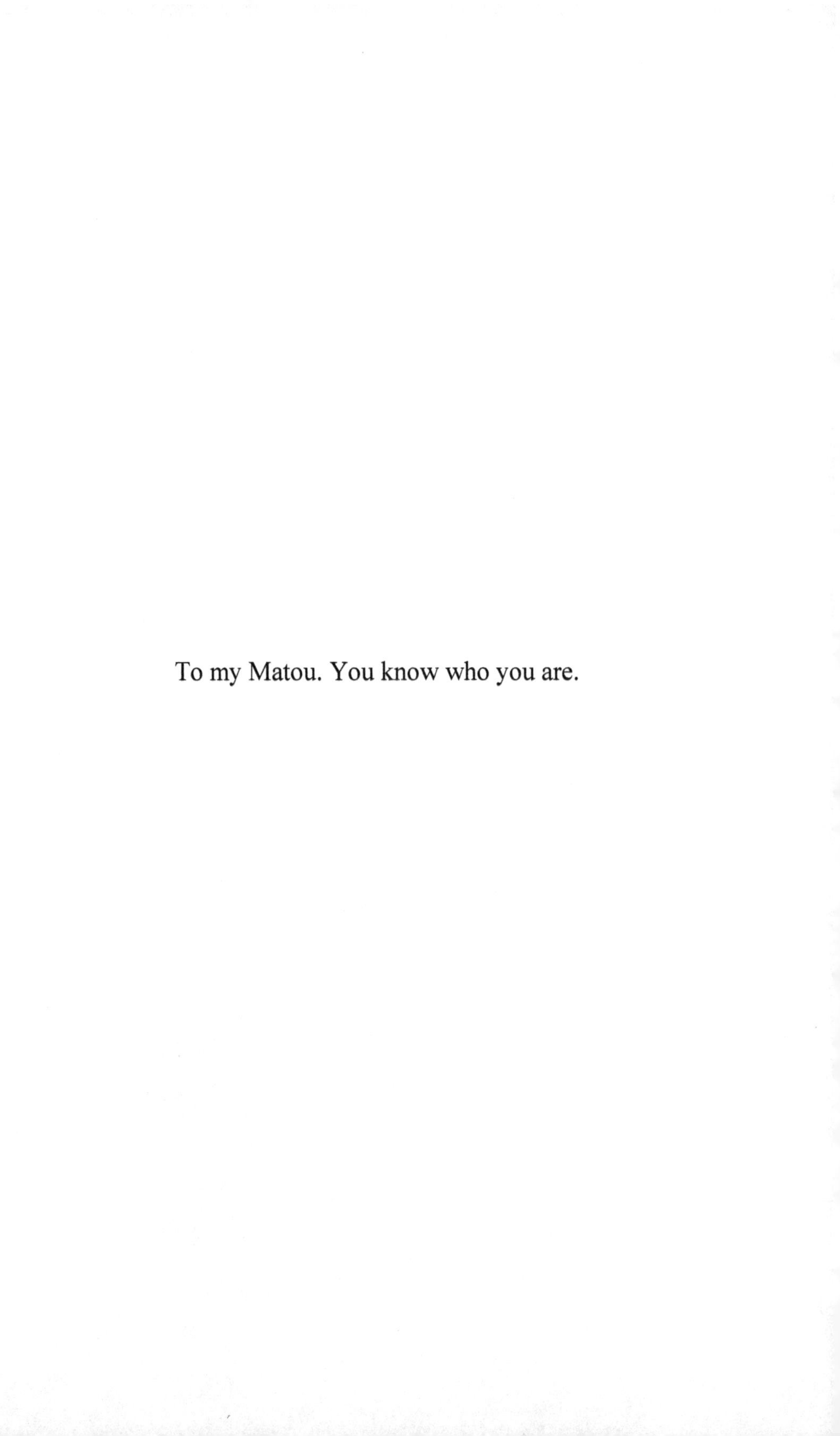

To my Matou. You know who you are.

"Come on, Claudia," Pliny Augur said, speaking to the flickering viewscreen transposed against his living room's far wall. "Let's get together, be siblings for once for Jupiter's sake."

His younger sister looked down her nose at him, her lips almost turning into a sneer. She shook her head, blond curls bouncing around her thin face. Like the rest of her, they were fake. "Be seen in public, with *you*?"

Pliny sighed, his slight shoulders slumping. "Saturnalia only comes once a year. Since Mom and Dad…" he trailed off. "You know."

"I know? Is that all you can say?" Claudia pinched a curl between her fingers, pulled and let it spring back into position. "Of course I *know*. I was there, by Juno. You have no idea what I saw."

"I didn't mean … We should move on with our lives, together, it's been years." Pliny said.

"Have fun." Claudia's face blinked out of existence, leaving only the blank wall in Pliny's small apartment. Pliny shook his head, his eyes seeking the bust of Jupiter that stood in the corner. What would Jupiter do when confronted with a long-standing issue with his sister? Find some hapless maiden? Pliny smirked, but quickly extinguished it. If the Imperial Pantheon caught him thinking like that, he'd be sent in for re-education. At best. He didn't bother considering the worst. Everyone knew heretics were disposed of. Quickly. The Pantheon didn't lie.

If Pliny could have one wish in this world, this planet of Roma IV with its crescent of island continents and paradise-like climate, it would be to heal the rift between him and his sister. Friends aside, she was all he had in this world.

He pushed the thoughts from his mind. Thinking was not his chosen pastime. Games and a good evening out were more his style.

"By Diana, I'll go alone," he said.

He strode by his nude sculpture of Venus, which was painted in rich tones of red and purple with tumbling waves of black hair. The market wasn't going to wait. He quickly commanded his psionic home automation system to take a neural backup of his memories and mind. Just in case. The dissidents were becoming bolder in recent months.

Pliny squared his shoulders and walked into his room, not bothering to turn on the lights. He knew the exact positions of every piece of furniture, from the too-soft bed to his cheap plastic wardrobes designed to look like granite. He threw open the door to his closet, withdrawing a simple green tunic. The closet was orderly, save the crumpled black toga that lay in the corner. It hadn't moved since he'd torn it off after his parents' funeral. He couldn't bring himself to touch the accursed thing. He shook his head and gently closed the door, sealing the memories of his tears with it. Saturnalia was only one week a year, and he was going to enjoy it. With, or without his sister.

Chapter 1

The annual Saturnalia market bustled in the Caesarea district, the cacophony of street vendors' shuffled footsteps and loud cries filled the air. The sun's intense rays beat down upon the sandy ground. The marketplace was abuzz with life—peddlers in bright tunics hocking their wares, trinkets depicting the creatures of myth, like the centaur and Minotaur, and holy idols to ladies in fine silks and shabby beggars alike.

It was a rare spectacle, as most shopping was done from the privacy and safety of home. Pliny Augur was well aware of the risks of being outside in a crowded area, and Pliny was happy to have had the foresight to take a precautionary memory-download as a contingency. His simple sandals were gritty and the dirt was clumping between his sweaty toes. A crown of thinning brown hair graced his head. Terrorist attacks had become more frequent recently, targeting party goers and open events. Pliny sighed as he perused the collection of icons before him, trying to decide if he wanted the larger gold-plated icon of Jupiter set in all his glory, or a smaller pure gold symbol of a simple lightning bolt. Pliny turned the symbol representing dedication to Jupiter in his hands, pondering why only the Gods were allowed to be depicted in art here on Roma IV. Grit was everywhere, even on the idol's polished surface. He badly wanted to leave and forget trying to mend his relationship with his devout sister.

"Pure gold, that one," the dealer said, his voice mushy through a mouth missing many teeth. Deep wrinkles cut lines across his skin. Pliny wondered why the man hadn't invested in rejuvenation therapy. "Unless the customer would prefer one set in platinum?"

"Gold will do," Pliny said. "I don't like my sister that much." He winked, though at this moment he meant it.

"You know what they say, 'the bigger the idol the better the luck.'"

Pliny sighed and readied his thumb to press against the terminal in the merchant's hand. "Indeed."

"Get down!" a voice shouted before a collective gasp erupted from the assembled crowd. Then, screams. Pliny was jostled from behind, then from the front. He wrapped his arms around himself, idol still in his grip.

The sudden quiet was broken by bellows of gunfire, and the furious weaponry bore down on the market. Pliny's eyes went wide and he dropped to his knees, reaching for the perceived safety of the parched earth. The weapon fire found him first, and the kinetic bullet kissed his skull, filling his field of view with red. His ears rang and the skin and bone of his head were ablaze in pain. He fell to the ground, with the idol of Jupiter still clutched in his hand.

***

Pliny only sensed glimpses of what followed, jumbled through a mask of pain and the haze of scrambled sensations and thoughts. Rough hands on his shoulders, dragging him away. The peddler prying his idol from Pliny's deadened hand and a twist of his powerless outstretched thumb. Pressure on the back of his head, while someone wiped the blood and pale dust from his eyes. A black sphere seemed to rise up and separate all of these events. The black wall of death. It was immersed in a red halo, its luminescence burning into his sightless eyes with light twisting around its edges. Bright red jets erupted from the poles. Dread filled what little of him remained. *Was this death, the Gates of Pluto opened up to me?* came a singular muddied thought.

***

Pliny awoke to find himself in a beige recovery room, his green tunic replaced by a blue hospital gown. The back of his head was awash in agony, icicles shooting through his brain, leaving the ache of frost burn in its wake. It hurt to think, but he realized he must have had a neuronal replacement procedure to still be alive after a direct hit from a kinetic rifle.

Am I still myself? he wondered. It was a question that had kept philosophers arguing for centuries—does brain regrowth cause the soul to dissipate, or was it simply downloading old memories into regrown tissues? Pliny would have been the first to argue it didn't matter. Who cared about philosophy when there was wine to drink at Aurora's pub?

He rubbed his eyes and looked around. Facing him was a meter-high holographic display showing his vitals. The sharp colors hurt his eyes, and every ping that followed each heartbeat stabbed into his ears. Still, he scanned the screen. Heart rate, blood pressure, neuronal activity, healing nanobot status. All seemed, to him, to be operating well. Not that he knew what that was, his technical and scientific knowledge was limited to his work. To the left of the screen was a network of tubes and leads that served to keep him alive. To the right was an empty chair, and a bland beige door.

"What happened?" he managed to croak, not expecting an answer, as no person was present.

"You were shot during the Saturnalia Marketplace terrorist attack two days ago," a robotic voice replied.

"How bad?"

"The majority of your cranium was destroyed," the voice intoned, "and a total reconstruction of your brain and skull was initiated at the picoscopic level by specialized nanobots."

"I am a machine, then?" he asked, dreading the answer.

"You remain Pliny Augur, as you were before."

That … thing from before haunted him. "But who am I? Am I just an amalgamation of flesh and machine? Are my thoughts still my own?" Pliny's tongue was stiff, but he had to know the answer.

"That query is beyond the scope of my programming. You must rest."

Pliny closed his eyes, letting the darkness wash over him once more. The pain behind his eyes subsided to a low hum, though the constant pinging noise of the machine continued to assail his ears. Pliny willed his heart to stop so his ears could be soothed, but the damnable thumping would not cease.

It was the darkness he'd sensed between life and death that now haunted him. What was that space? Was it still there, waiting for him beyond the veil of consciousness? Or, was he dead?

The mystery of it pursued him, taunted him, until death's sister, sleep, finally enveloped him.

Chapter 2

Pliny stretched, letting his feet touch the floor for the first time since his arrival at the hospital. The lights still hurt his eyes, so he squinted momentarily before deciding to accept the pain. He braced himself, expecting the cold white tile to somehow feel different, or that he would fall through it into oblivion. To his surprise, the familiar cold sensation pressed against the soles of his feet, and Roma IV's gravity still pulled against him. He untied his hospital gown, letting it slide to the floor. He turned to the bed, and grasped the rough brown linen tunic the hospital had provided, as his own clothes had been ruined on the day of the attack. He moved his hand to the back of his head. He still had his hair, he noted with satisfaction. Not that he'd consider the regrowth procedure—he'd turned down the opportunity for that years ago in favor of looking more unique.

"It's only been a day since I woke up, are you sure I'm ready to go home?" he asked the empty room, waiting for the omnipresent AI tender to answer him.

"Your reconstruction was a trivial procedure and only required a three night regrowth period," the machine replied.

"Was my family notified?" he asked. *Or anyone?*

"Yes. Your sister, Claudia Augur, is waiting for you outside.

You may join her. Have a pleasant day." The voice winked out and there was an audible click from the direction of the door.

He crept toward the beige door, not looking back to the messy bed or the monitor. He turned the handle, and entered into an equally beige hallway, punctuated by closed doors and glaring lights. Pliny suppressed the urge to wince. People in blue coveralls power walked down the hall with a sure destination in mind, and others in street clothes idled outside the doors without purpose. Claudia was one of the latter. Slender and fine-featured, she was a woman of about twenty five. She looked at him, her frown bursting into sharp laughter. Pliny's eyebrows raised. This wasn't like their last meeting, not at all.

"So, they can glue your brains back together, but they can't fix your bald spot!" she quipped, then frowned as she further scrutinized his features. His cheeks heated.

Pliny's hand reflexively moved to his head. His hair was, indeed, still thinning. He'd already known this, but having it pointed out by Claudia made it more real. "Damn it Claudia, I almost died and that's all you can say?" he asked.

"You didn't *almost* die, silly. Besides, what would I do without my big brother?"

"Something very stupid, rest assured," Pliny replied. He cocked his head. "Why are you so happy to see me?"

She shrugged. "Something like this, it makes you think. Sometimes about things that shouldn't be considered," she began. She shook her head. "You're right, we are the only family we have. I'm willing to rethink our relationship."

Pliny blinked. "Rethink?"

"Don't hurt yourself pondering that. Just enjoy the moment," she said, chuckling.

Pliny smiled. It was almost like it had been, before the incident. Before the pain.

They moved through the halls of the hospital, exchanging jabs as though nothing life-changing had happened, and the past several years of mutual antagonism hadn't occurred. Pliny was reassured by Claudia's presence; her cheerful demeanor radiated like the sun's rays. However, the darkness that had found its way into Pliny's soul remained. *Could it be an after effect of the surgery,* he wondered. *Or, something deeper inside me that has emerged? Have I changed?*

Upon exiting the hospital, the sun warmed Pliny's exposed skin. A light breeze ruffled his rough tunic. The air smelled real, like that of a warm summer's day with a touch too much humidity. But, there was a *wrongness* to it, a wrongness he could not quite define. Around them, people carried on as usual. The world hadn't changed.

Claudia grabbed him by the arm and led him toward her car. The vehicle hovered about thirty centimeters off the ground, and was the shape of a bean and the color of Jupiter's lightning. Pliny climbed inside and sat on the soft, plush passenger seat. Of course it was purple. Claudia would paint the world purple, if she could. A holographic screen floated before the windshield, its green projection a harsh contrast to the street and the interior of the vehicle. Claudia directed the car to drive to Pliny's home and then pressed the engage button. She leaned back in her chair before scowling at him.

"Is something on your mind, brother?" she asked, turning to face him. "You haven't insulted my intelligence, choice in life partners, or even the fact that I have all of my hair," she said. "Could it be they actually added a brain in that head of yours?"

"I've just been preoccupied with a few things," he admitted. Should he say anything?

"Tell tell," she said. "Tell me everything."

"It's just, I was dead. It was a darkness like I've never experienced before. I need some time to process, to meditate on it." There was nothing else he could say. That was the only way he could know who, or what, he was.

"You're alive now, and that's what matters. I wouldn't let a corpse in my car," she said.

"But you let your second boyfriend's girlfriend in," he said, forcing a smile. "Or is that partner now? I can never keep track of your love life."

"Now, that's the brother I know and loathe," she replied.

Pliny looked out the window, drawing in the normalcy of it all. Could he get used to being alive again?

Chapter 3

Pliny stepped into his small apartment, turning on the light with a singular mental command. It had been more expensive, but psychic integration for his apartment had been worth the investment, especially now that he owed his life and mind to his mental backup interface. His sandals slapped on tile floor. The interior temperature was kept constant based on his mood and needs, but today, the place was cold, almost uncomfortably so. His walls were covered in decorations, all based on the Imperial Pantheon's approved list of idols. There was a nude plaster cast of a three dimensional relief of Jupiter, the bearded Father of the Gods, lightning bolt in hand. Another was Minerva the wise, with her scrolls and shield. Mars too had a place on his walls, the armor-clad god of war charging into battle. Pliny examined each in turn, wondering if these gods looked down on their followers or were even aware of them. He banished the thought as a chill shot down his spine. He hoped the Pantheon wasn't watching his thoughts, not that there were many of interest.

Pliny willed the holo-entertainment screen to turn on, and took a seat in the only gray armchair in the room, a recliner. A couch dominated the far wall, but Pliny only used the leather behemoth for naps.

"Might as well see what happened," he muttered.

He activated the screen, and searched for information on the Saturnalia market terrorist attack. There were numerous sources of information. He chose The Daily Thunder, a reliable and usually unbiased Pantheon-approved news source. According to the Thunder, the gunmen had been killed and the Imperial judge ordered that they not be resuscitated. Of the over 100 injured, 43 were critical, and there were five fatalities. Such was the cost of poverty. Had those people been able to afford a psychic integration unit, they would be alive now. Pliny shook his head.

Pliny flicked off the screen and reclined in his chair. There he was, a statistic. A number to be parroted about, and used as ammunition for Emperor Vespasian VII to curtail yet more civil liberties and extend the curfew.

Unlike the terrorists and heretics, Pliny wasn't overly troubled by curfews and liberties, so long as he could have his drinks at Aurora's, chase women and watch his holo-entertainment screen. But, something had changed in him, something immutable and indescribable. He meditated on it, focusing on his breath, trying to will the troubling darkness he'd felt when he died back to himself. It would not come.

There he sat, for what seemed like hours, meditating, napping, and staring into space. Behind every state of consciousness the darkness hovered like a ghost. Was he forever changed by a bullet to the head, or was there a deeper truth tiptoeing at the edges of his unconscious mind? He sighed.

He stood, deciding that a walk back to the market was just what he needed. Checking the time, he realized it was almost curfew, so the trip would have to wait.

Instead, Pliny opted to call his sister. He had just seen her, but perhaps she could help him make sense of it all. He willed the screen to call her, and waited for her to answer. Unlike him, she didn't have a psionic entertainment system installed in her home.

Claudia's face appeared on the screen, her back against the pastel yellow living room wall. The black tip of a lightning bolt hung over her head like a warning. The holo-screen droned on in the background, though no intelligible words could be discerned. "Hello, big brother. Back for more abuse?" she asked.

"Actually, I need to talk. Serious talk. Are you alone?" He swallowed. He never knew which of her life partners could be around, and while he was certain they were people of quality, he didn't want them knowing his business.

Claudia looked beyond the camera and said "Shoo. Go to the bedroom or the kitchen; I need privacy," she said, and after a moment she continued, "Okay, we're alone, what's so important that my primary partner can't hear? Oh yes, you don't even *have* a partner. You wouldn't understand."

Pliny sighed inwardly. His perpetual bachelorhood had always been a point of contention between them. "When our parents were killed back in the Red Mood Riots, did you feel a darkness inside you?" he asked. She'd been close to them when they'd died. Maybe death was a presence that could find its way into your mind and soul?

"Of course! It was like there was a void inside me that couldn't be filled. What kind of question is that?" she replied. "I was there, by Jupiter! I almost died too!"

"A very real one. Ever since they regrew my brain I sense this darkness that I can't shake, or identify."

"Sounds like they put you back together wrong, or it's yet another bout of your usual self-pity," she said.

"No, this is something else," he began, drawing the words out. "I saw something while I was dead, and it haunts me," Pliny said.

"Silly, you can't see anything when you're dead. It's probably just an artifact of the reconstruction surgery, go look it up. Maybe it was put there to entertain you."

"All right, I'll look it up," he said.

"Oh, one more thing," she said, holding up a finger.

"What?"

"There's an awesome documentary on black holes just coming up on Minerva. Maybe you should investigate some real darkness. Expand your mind for once."

He sighed. "Thanks, sis, thanks for listening."

"Love you too" she said, before severing the link.

Left alone, he changed the channel to Minerva, deciding he'd numb his mind with some insipid documentary before going to bed. He put his feet up and had a bottle of wine floated to his side table. It was time to lose himself.

Chapter 4

Pliny set the book down on the weathered wooden table, and mulled over what he'd just read. After watching the documentary on black holes, Pliny had become fascinated by the enigmatic stellar objects. Accretion discs, event horizons, and space-time. Concepts he'd never heard of before in his life as a pico-electronics technician. A singularity in the universe, like a hole in existence. He'd heard the term black hole in school, but never cared enough to find out more. *Where could that hole lead?* he wondered. Another reality? Nowhere? He shuddered at the thought. Nowhere seemed worse than death. At least, in death, you'd enter Pluto's realm as a petitioner.

The library's holdings were limited, but the ancient books were more accessible than modern literature, most of which was censored by the Imperial Pantheon. Pliny sniffed the pages, taking in the scent of millennium-old paper. It was heady, and intoxicating in its own right.

He was surrounded by books of every color of the rainbow. Tall shelves rose to the library's high ceiling. The smell of ozone permeated the air, a by-product of the shielding protecting the books from the cruel ministrations of time.

A nasal voice spoke from behind him. "Are you done with

that? The books can only be outside the shields for a few hours at a time before losing their protective cover."

"Oh, yes, please," Pliny replied.

The librarian's spindly hands dutifully gathered up the books that had been removed from their safe haven and dropped the stasis field for just long enough to deposit the books back in their allotted space, then reactivating it. Pliny was left alone with his thoughts and the notes he'd taken on his trusty psionic watch.

He'd sift through the mentally-recorded notes later, as pure recorded thoughts could be cluttered with extraneous garbage, daydreams, or worse still, forbidden thoughts. He didn't know what the Pantheon's stance on black holes was, but the librarian's sour face had told him all he'd needed to know about her opinion.

Pliny stood and strode through the maze of high-walled book shelves to the exit, past stern-faced librarians. As Pliny exited the building, he realized there still was one place left to go.

***

The Temple of Pluto was a towering behemoth of a building, windowless and the color of obsidian. A swirling black portal marked the entrance, and Pliny shuddered in spite of himself, remembering the black wall of death he'd seen when he died only days before. This is where the cremated remains of Roma IV's dead were interred, the temple serving as both a place of worship and a mausoleum.

Pliny grit his teeth as he entered the building, trying not to let memories of grief wash over him. The death of his parents in a stampede of rioters five years before was still a fresh wound in his soul, and he avoided visiting their niche for that reason. Claudia had survived the incident, but not without emotional scars of her own.

The interior was as gloomy and intimidating as the exterior. The furniture was fashioned with ebony native to Roma IV. A deep orange holo-display hovered in front of him, directing him to various services. Pliny walked past the screen and into the office beyond, feeling the screen's electric field tickle his skin and add a slight buzz to his curly hair.

A priest greeted him. Wearing a black toga, the man was the very image of death. An albino, his ghost-white skin and red eyes fixed on Pliny the moment he walked in.

"Good evening, I am Deathseer Antonius," the man said. "Welcome to the Temple of Pluto. Are you in need of a guide for the dead? Funerary services? An advance purchase of a niche?"

Pliny stumbled for a moment before replying. "No, I want to talk about something else."

"What would that be?" Antonius smiled, his white teeth flashed against the pure ivory of his skin.

"I want to talk about death," Pliny replied, his palms sweaty.

The priest motioned to the tall-backed chair that sat across from his empty desk. "Of course, what would you like to know, petitioner?"

"What is death, exactly?"

"It's a gate through which all beings must pass," was the reply. "Even the Ohm, the great trees of the Herculean forests on the island of Concordia become husks, remnants of their former glory."

"Can a person see this gate?" Pliny asked.

"To my knowledge, very few people alive have seen the Gates of Pluto's realm. To do so would be a great blessing," he said, chuckling. "I would love to see it. A place of infinite dissolution and evaporation of the spirit. A great nothingness. Ah, to be broken down by the will of a God." The priest looked to be in a moment of rapturous pleasure just by the thought.

Pliny's stomach turned over and put his parents' death from his mind, remembering his true purpose. "I need to talk about something I saw last week, if that's possible?" Pliny asked, avoiding the priest's red gaze.

"Go ahead," was the reply, hands folded across his ghostly visage. "I do enjoy the chance to speak with the populace from time to time."

"I sustained a major head injury requiring extensive reconstruction," he began, before sucking in a deep breath and continuing, "I saw a wall, a black wall, coming toward me, edged in red. It looked like death. I… I can't forget it, turn back from it. It haunts me. What did I see?"

The priest's smile turned into a frown. "So, you had a vision of death while you were being resuscitated?"

"So it seemed. It left an impression on me, I have to know," Pliny said, the strength returning to his voice.

"Ah," the man said, smiling. "Sometimes a person sees the Obsidian Gates of Pluto's realm during such an experience. We interpret this as a blessing. You have been most fortunate. You should consider serving the Temple of Pluto. A blessed soul would make an excellent Deathseer." He then lowered his voice. "You may have the gift of sight beyond worlds, something not seen in ages."

There was no way Pliny would consider enlisting to become a Deathseer. It was so … chilling and morose to even visit this place. Sight or no sight, he was going to continue his old life. "So I'm blessed by…Pluto? It seems odd to be blessed by the god of Death," Pliny said. "Are there any prayers I should offer? But, if it's all the same to you, I'll stick with civilian life."

"Pluto chooses his candidates with great care. Death is a great mystery, you see. None have crossed the river Styx and returned to tell us of the great wastes. Sometimes, we mortals must take what we can get. Refer to the Pantheon's scriptures, they will guide you in the appropriate devotions. Be sure to appreciate the shadow when the time is right," Antonius said.

"Indeed," Pliny replied. "The shadow?"

"Pluto is best venerated in shadow. Make your shrine in a corner that receives no sunlight, and ensure that you burn no candles at the base of it. Pluto planted the ground with gems, so make sure the alter is inlaid with precious metals and gems of good quality. If you do this, Pluto will be appeased and perhaps you will return to me with more visions."

"I see. I suppose I needed to redecorate," Pliny said with a sigh. Another shrine? Where would he put his favorite satyr corner piece?

"It is for the best. Is there anything else I can offer you today?" Antonius asked.

"No, thank you. You've been most helpful," Pliny lied.

"I'd offer you a blessing, but I think you've already been touched by the Lord of Death and that will more than suffice."

Pliny left the temple of Pluto more confused than before, in search of an answer that may not exist.

Unless he discovered an answer for himself.

Chapter 5

"It's simple, Claudia," Pliny said. Claudia's face was suspended in the center of his living room, while he sat in his recliner. The most notable change in his decor was the removal of the majority of the icons of the Pantheon on his walls. "I saw it, a singularity. Like the black holes from that documentary last week, remember?"

She rolled her eyes. "That's the last time I recommend a documentary to you. Even a child could figure out that you saw the Gates to Pluto's Realm. The damned Underrealm. You should be buying lottery tickets and an altar, instead you're raving about black holes and spiritual oneness."

"You don't understand," he began, holding his hands outstretched, before Claudia cut him off.

"Look, I'm telling you to take the night and think about what you're saying, Pliny. We are not all connected by a singular force, and even if we were, it would not be by a singularity. It would be the divine will of the Gods. There. Case closed. Go make your amends to Jupiter before the Imperial Pantheon hears of this heresy," she said, scowling. Her curls bounced as she shook her head. "How do we know they're not listening right now?" she said in a hushed tone.

She closed the link, leaving Pliny alone with his thoughts once again. He pondered what she'd said. She said that there was no force that could connect the teeming masses of humanity from all colonized worlds. How could that not be obvious? He ran his hand over his closely-cut tight curls. Had part of himself been left dead on the sandy ground of the Saturnalia marketplace, thus making him partly dead? If so, that would explain how he could have seen it.

Pliny frantically paced his small apartment, from his utilitarian sparsely furnished bedroom to his kitchen, with its faux-marble counter tops, hanging steel utensils and a flat black cooking surface. Pliny had made the kitchen as fancy as he could afford. He enjoyed entertaining the dates and friends he would invite back to his home.

Perhaps that was the key. Out. He could go out and tell people he met about his experience and theory, and get some unbiased feedback. Claudia, for all her merits, was a bit of a zealot. There was only one way to find out the truth. His truth. The Pantheon surely had more important battles to fight than against one man's inquiries into Pluto's realm.

****

Pliny mingled in the crowd. The scent of alcohol hung in the air. He nursed a bubbly purple Roma Sunrise, his drink of choice. He especially liked swirling the glass and watching the small fireworks that exploded with each collision of the ice cubes that floated at the top. The social event wasn't quite what he'd had in mind, but it provided an opportunity to find intellectual and influential people. The banquet hall had a high ceiling and was replete with Roman-style pillars, and a fountain in the image of a nude Venus pouring water into a pool at the center. Pliny had been able to parlay his way into this event by portraying himself as a modern day philosopher. Which he was, in a manner of speaking. He'd conveniently left out his lack of a permit for his studies and efforts.

Pliny walked up to a young man in his thirties with dark skin, chiseled features and a head of long, blond hair bound in braids. Thanks to advances in life-prolonging technology, youth now extended to around seventy years of age. Pliny couldn't place the man's true age, not that these things mattered. Pliny held out a hand, and introduced himself. "Pliny Augur, philosopher. And yourself?"

"Gaius Titius, starship artisan and trainee pilot," the man said, grasping Pliny's forearm. "You don't see many philosophers in these parts anymore. What's left to philosophize about? And better yet, who cares?"

"Well," began Pliny, bracing himself for another rebuttal, "I concern myself with the oneness of humanity and questions of an astronomical nature. And as to caring, that's up to you. I am simply looking for interesting conversation. If you are *open* to a round," he said, the last sentence being a type of code he'd discovered intellectual circles using to denote trust, of a sort.

"Always time for a round," Gaius said in reply, ushering Pliny away from the crowd. "I've never thought much about it, we've all been pretty different as a people since Nero II splintered us from the Terran Federation two millennia ago. And, let's not forget Horus III and their heretical Pantheon. Humanity isn't terribly united, I'm afraid."

"I've come up with a theory that may sound outlandish, but, rest assured, I've done my research." Pliny swallowed. Was his sister right, was it heresy?

"This should be good, might as well hear you while we're having a round," the man said, taking a glance over his shoulder. Pliny looked over. There was nobody there.

"Let's begin," Pliny said, wetting his lips, "by saying that all humans die. This is a given, even without life-extending technology."

"Right," the man said, checking his watch. "And?"

"I have died, and seen its black gates. But, it was not a construct like a gate, rather, it was a sphere, a complete void!" Pliny replied.

"A void? Then what of Pluto's Gates? The river Styx and the Boatman?" Gaius crossed his arms over his broad chest.

"I've taken them as stories. Remember Nero II's founding address?" Pliny asked.

"Yes, 'to bring back the old ways and Gods through faith alone and sweep all before us.' I know the dogma." Gaius said. "This is intriguing and all, but …" he said, training off.

"Then," Pliny said, looking carefully around to see if anyone was listening, "Perhaps we should continue this conversation somewhere more private?"

"We can use my office, another day I suppose," Gaius said, flipping through the calendar holographically projected above his watch. Pliny did the same, slightly dismayed by his obvious lack of appointments. "How about in the evening, at 18 hundred in four days? That leaves time for us to get home before the curfew at 22 hundred."

"That is acceptable," Pliny said, dialing the date and time onto the circular calendar.

"See you then, Pliny," Gaius said, patting Pliny on the shoulder before vanishing into the crowd.

Pliny could barely contain his excitement. He considered approaching a few others at this function, but instead went home to bed. He couldn't risk breaching the fast-approaching curfew, after all. Or alerting the Pantheon. Not before he had his theory straight.

Chapter 6

Pliny walked through the door of his workplace—Minotaur Nanoelectronics—as soon as curfew allowed, and was greeted by his employer. The sterile white lab was graced by many workbenches with identical tool kits affixed to the cubicle walls. His boss, Germanicus Flavius, was a sweaty man in the throes of a mid-life crisis. He refused to reveal his age, but Pliny would give him at least 125, though his colleagues sometimes guessed as high as 150. Pliny idly wondered when the man would give up and retire to a seaside villa somewhere far away. Preferably on another planet.

"Pliny! I heard what happened. Are you okay?" The man's small eyes peered at Pliny's skull as though he was trying to see the grafts of new flesh.

"Good as new, more or less," Pliny began, but quickly added: "thank the Gods for medical reconstruction. I'm back to normal, and you won't need to hire a new employee."

Germanicus barked a laugh. "Still got your winning sense of humor, I see. Well, get to work. We're behind and need all hands on deck to keep up with the festival next week. It's good to have my best employee back, but next time you need a week off, I'm taking it out of your vacation time!" Germanicus clapped Pliny on the back and walked away.

Pliny nodded and headed over to his station, dodging concerned looks and eye contact. Something was wrong. Him, here, away from his research and notes. But, he had a job, and he couldn't investigate what had happened to him without it. The Gods hadn't come back and eliminated the need for credits. He picked up his electron scanning goggles and put his mind into his work. The picobots shimmered as they entered his vision, vanishing as he picked one and began attaching pieces to it. A silver spindly leg and clay-like arms completed the prototype. He set it to mass-produce other picobots of its type, taking care to make sure that their containment wasn't breached. An escaped picobot could cause mayhem and begin attempting to convert equipment, desks and even workers into smaller bots. It was simple enough to keep them under control, and a simple task was what Pliny needed to stay focused. It was all he could do, as he tried to remove the swirling dark sphere from the forefront of his thoughts.

***

Pliny leaned back and deactivated his goggles, allowing his vision to return to normal. He focused on the distant clock, grounding himself to the moment. It was lunchtime, and his group of friends would be waiting for him. Pushing himself away from his table, he contemplated skipping out. How could he explain what he saw to skeptics, or worse, believers with no critical thought. But, the hollow in his stomach compelled him to go to the cafeteria and meander among the metal seats until he arrived at his usual space.

Greeted by awkward nods and half-smiles from colleagues he

barely knew as he walked, Pliny felt even more lost. Was it pity? Was it concern about their own mortality? He couldn't be certain. When he first entered the sterile metal-lined cafeteria, he laid eyes on his work friend, Felix, a young man of thirty with a mop of red curls on his head. Felix waved Pliny over as Pliny picked up the tray holding his usual lunch, a large bowl of dodo soup.

Pliny barely had sat down on his chair before the questions started. "What was it like? Were you really dead? Did you meet Pluto?" The words tumbled out of Felix's mouth almost as fast as he could articulate.

"Whoa, there! Let me at least take a mouthful first, being dead made me pretty hungry," Pliny said.

"I know, sorry, but I've never known anyone who was reconstructed so completely before. Most come back with bits and pieces of memories and personality missing." Felix narrowed his eyes and picked up a fork.

Pliny suppressed a shudder and brought a spoon of soup to his lips. "It's a strange thing, coming back," he began before moving the soup past his lips, mentally comparing the briny broth to what he remembered. The memory was a match, like all the rest. Maybe he'd come back with more, rather than less? He let the broth sit on his tongue to buy him time before the next onslaught of questions. "I was really dead, as the certificate that I had to get to excuse my time off work indicates. Thank goodness for mind backups, right?"

"Right… maybe I should invest in one," Felix said.

"You don't have one? How do you leave the house?" Pliny replied.

"Sometimes there are other obligations that have to come first. But you didn't answer my questions."

Pliny took another spoonful and sighed. "Okay, I really guess you've never met a dead person before. It hurt. A lot. Like my whole head was on fire. They recreated all of it, right down to the bald spot." He stared into the mass of swirling noodles and vegetables.

"Why in Pluto's name do you keep the bald spot? Even I ponied up the cash to make that go away," Felix said. "Seriously, it makes you look like you're in your nineties."

"No good reason. It makes me feel more like an individual than a perfect plastic person."

"Ouch, that was below the belt, even for you Pliny."

Pliny smirked. Felix had his moments and Pliny enjoyed the banter. It kept his wits sharp, especially with the mind-numbing nature of his work and the relative mundane nature of his thoughts.

"I'll get you for that one," Felix added.

"I'm sure you will," Pliny replied.

"What about my other questions? Does Pluto have a secret handshake?"

"You know what," Pliny replied, "How about you come over for supper and I'll fill you in."

"Sounds great, I'll meet you at your desk after our shift."

Pliny nodded and went back to his now lukewarm soup. The rest of the usual crowd sat with them, and an awkward silence ensued. Pliny excused himself as soon as he finished eating and went back to his workbench. Germanicus was going to get some free extra labor this afternoon.

Chapter 7

Aelia Vellus walked through the Grand Chamber of the Temple of the Pantheon. The room was inlaid with vivid mosaics depicting past Emperors and scenes from the great scriptures. Six sculpted pillars of Atlas supported the high ceiling, which was painted with the constellations of the night sky. Aelia found her eyes drawn to the sculpted perfection of the nude Atlas. The strained muscles, the semblance of motion at every angle from which he was viewed. Aelia tried not to look at his loins, they made her blush and feel depraved. Why did the great figures of their history have no modesty? The chamber diminished her in the face of the Pantheon of Gods. The grandiosity of the great hall demonstrated Roma IV's desire to resurrect and service the divine. Aelia wondered if the Gods would ever return to them, and, more importantly, reward them for their faithful service. But, today was just another day for High Inquisitor Marcia Canius and the Imperial Pantheon's other servants. Aelia made her way to the back of the chamber, leaving her musings about Atlas behind as she entered the High Inquisitor's antechamber. Aelia swallowed nervously, in spite of herself, and bunched up her black robes in white knuckled hands to strengthen her resolve. Her small face was a mask of worry and her short stature was dwarfed by the lavish setting. She cast her green eyes downwards.

Aelia breathed deeply and entered the chamber, which was brightly lit and lacking in religious idolatry, a stark contrast to the severeness and pomp of the grand chamber. A large ebony desk dominated the room, and a range of stasis-protected bookshelves lined the back wall. The room hummed to the tune of stasis, and a solitary figure sat in a chair before her. Aelia dropped to one knee. "Mistress," she said, bowing her head.

"Rise, my child," a soft but firm voice replied.

Aelia rose to her feet, the echo of the powerful voice ringing in her ears. Her heart raced. The figure was the High Inquisitor herself, her gray locks contrasting sharply against an almost ageless face, her red cowl drawing a stark divergence between the woman's hair and blood red clothing. Aelia suspected that the woman had allowed herself to gray, despite the available age-reversing treatments and the near limitless coffers of the Pantheon. The gray made the Mistress all the more imposing and powerful. Aelia said nothing, and waited for her elder to speak.

"How proceeds the Claudius case?" the High Inquisitor asked.

"I have had him put to the question," Aelia replied. "He would not produce a confession through standard methods of interrogation. Regrettable, but I find that pain is an excellent motivator."

"I see," came the reply.

Aelia swallowed. Had she done something wrong? Protocol had been obeyed to the letter.

"Effective immediately, you're being reassigned." Marcia declared then, her small eyes narrowing.

Aelia's head hung. The Claudius assignment was the opportunity to truly begin her career. Breaking a dissident leader would elevate her above her peers and propel her to new heights.

"Worry not, child, I have other designs for you." Long fingernails tapped on the desk.

"What would those be, High Inquisitor?"

"I have word of a heretic, a philosopher of sorts, who has surfaced in the wake of the Saturnalia market attack this past month. You know better than most how serious this is."

Aelia nodded, waiting for the rest.

"You are young, and attractive. I need you to get close. Find a way in the door and see how far this heretic has poisoned our world and faith."

"I understand, Mistress. Where do I begin?"

＊

The trip to the Caesarea district had been uneventful, and Aelia's driver left her at her rented room—a temporary hovel that would distance her from the Imperial Pantheon. It was a small and dingy space, one small bedroom and a kitchenette were all it contained. However, her abode had been outfitted with a psionic mental backup unit. If she were to perish, they would still have their necessary evidence and her work could be continued with minimal time lost. Its other implied function was to train a replacement inquisitor. The notion of requiring a replacement was distasteful to her, so she cast the thought from her mind. This man, this Pliny Augur, would fall into her net soon enough and earn her a seat at her Mistress's right hand.

First, she would need to retrace Pliny's steps, starting with the source of the allegations. A murmur here, a rumor there, all would add fuel to her fire.

"What could cause heresy on such a basic level?" she asked out loud, incredulous at how one person could so easily stray, especially an educated citizen like Pliny. She gazed at a three-dimensional holograph taken from his online presence. Average enough. Strange receding hairline, not particularly well-built, but nor was he a soft weakling. She doubted he would pose much of a challenge to her—heretics seldom did once exposed and punished.

She sat at her rough wooden table and sipped on a glass of water before willing the interface to activate. She needed to do her due diligence before beginning. It was going to be a long night.

Aelia smiled. She was going to enjoy this hunt.

Chapter 8

Pliny walked into a room filled with his peers—a gathering to discuss the nature of the human condition. Within the Pantheon's accepted limits, of course. It was a venue open to the public with a small cover charge, set in a large conference room. Holographic posters by various philosophers shimmered along the white walls, headlined by esoteric titles that made Pliny suspect that none of them knew what they were really talking about, or what they themselves even meant. He had confidence and certainty on his side. The rest of the room was dim and shabby, something rented on a budget by underfunded colleges most likely. Suspended from ceiling projectors was a holographic display indicating where the programmed talks and speeches were to be held. The lineup did not appeal to Pliny, but he made a mental note to come back to subsequent meetings in case he changed his mind.

Pliny found himself drawn to an exhibit discussing the Oneness of Humanity. He was intrigued—could it be that humanity's nature was a universal constant, even a single teeming entity?

A voice cleared behind Pliny. Pliny turned to see a woman, smallish with red-streaked curly black hair. She certainly had the appearance of someone who would dabble in the intellectual fields. She wore a red floor-length dress that was bare at the shoulders and the fabric held a shimmer, likely from micro-crystals woven into the light fabric. "I see you like my poster," she began, and added: "I'm Tetra Antonius, a student here at the University of Roma downtown."

"I'm Pliny, and yes, your work is fascinating."

"Why thank you!" she exclaimed, motioning to the image. "I tried to focus my research on a more philosophical than religious viewpoint. I believe this approach makes it more relevant and less heretical than other investigations into the nature of humanity and our connectivity as individual beings."

"A wise precaution, I'm sure." Pliny stroked his chin and considered adding highlights to his hair.

"Anything to keep the Pantheon from breaking down my door, right?" She looked from side to side. "One of my professors was nabbed out of class when I was a freshman. Just, gone. Screaming and pleading. You can't be too careful."

Pliny swallowed and nodded, wondering if he was safe. Tetra wouldn't have been granted a spot at this group if she was a blasphemer, would she? "What saved you?" he inquired.

"The Executor in charge didn't consider a group of eighteen year olds to be indoctrinated. Anyhow, I'm very careful. That could have been me, you know." Her eyes drifted back to her poster.

"I'm so sorry you went through that. Was his work your inspiration?" he asked.

"No, but I see things… differently from other people. I see bonds, connections and the intimacy between others, if that makes sense. Naturally, I went into philosophy so I could have a better understanding of what humanity was really about."

"So you're a Seer?" Pliny asked.

"Not really, just an astute observer. I don't think a Seer has been born since Nero II decided to separate Roma IV from the Terran Federation to bring back the old Gods."

"Indeed, such a glorious decision indeed," Pliny said more loudly, in case anyone was listening. Pantheon spies could be anywhere, especially in a forum for fresh ideas. Lowering his voice, he mentioned, "I am also a philosopher of sorts, and I'd enjoy an exchange of ideas. Oneness has been on my mind a great deal lately, and I need someone grounded and bright to bounce ideas off of."

Tetra blushed. "You're too kind" she said, holding the back of her hand to her cheek. "Nobody's taken my work so seriously before, I'd love to have an intellectual exchange for once. Most people write me off because they find that my ideas are strange," she finished, choosing the final word carefully.

"Not to me," Pliny said, extending a hand. "Not ever."

She shook his hand and smiled. "Now, give me your coordinates and we can move right along with this discussion another time, when there's not such a crowd. I hate crowds."

Pliny pressed two fingers to his inner forearm, and a small holographic screen projected itself into the space above. Tetra did the same. "Until next time. Perhaps in three days time?" They exchanged contact information.

"Three days. No longer," she said, winking. "Now shoo, I'm getting a line."

Pliny left in search of other ideas, but little else was of interest in the room, especially not in the presentations done by the dried-up looking elders. Pliny idly wondered if he would become that stuffy when he reached such an age, the age where life-extending treatments were no longer possible and the natural order of things returned in force. *But you already were saved by life-extending treatments*, he thought to himself, which only served to heighten his existential crisis.

Pliny walked out of the building, almost bumping into a green-eyed woman in long gray robes. After excusing himself, he strode over to where his old hover car was parked, floating about a foot off of the ground. He unlocked it and climbed inside. A cute girl's contact and the possibility of some relevant philosophical debate? He couldn't get any luckier than that! He pushed her memories of the Pantheon's intercession in her freshman year from his mind. It couldn't happen to him.

He drove off into the night, his encounter with the woman in the gray robe already forgotten.

Chapter 9

Pliny was back at the library, this time examining religious texts. His desk was littered with old paper books, yellowed pages and their small lettering in the bright light of the room. A tiny holographic display containing his personal notes was hovering at the back of the desk. He'd set his cubicle to private mode, so he was left to his own devices with his research. It was unnerving floating in a black void, but he used the sensory deprivation of his surroundings to hone his thoughts. He was alone with the scent of paper, the hum of holography and the shuffling of tomes.

He wanted to determine the Imperial Pantheon's stance on alternative viewpoints on the fellowship of humanity, but was instead greeted by Jupiter's sexual misadventures, and trips across the River Styx by a greedy boatman. For a long time, Pliny had even carried two coins in his boot, just in case. He frowned, coming to a logical end. People were seen as individuals under the tyranny of an all-powerful Jupiter, his queen Juno, and the dead were sent to Pluto's realm for their eternal reward. He would have to study ancient philosophers from Old Terra, most of which were under lock and key and unavailable to the public. They were, however, available to someone with an academic background. He smiled, noting that he could ask Tetra for access when he contacted her later. He had done his due diligence in this trip to the library, and was not unprepared to face her intellectual prowess.

He sighed, closing his notes and looking over his shoulder before pressing a small red button to his left to alert the librarian that he was finished. The black walls of the cubicle vanished, bringing him back to reality. The towering bookshelves, the twinge of ozone, the murmur of conversation. It hit Pliny like an avalanche, and he sat there, blinking.

"Did you find what you need?" asked a woman who possessed an absurdly long neck and a collection of dirty blond curls cascaded down its length. She peered down a long nose at him, looking over his shoulder and peering at his notes.

"Just satisfying some curiosity. I'm looking to do some very inspired shopping for my sister's birthday. She needs a good gift," he replied with a wink, quickly deactivating his holo-screen.

"Jupiter always delivers, no matter the occasion. Just don't give her a set of copper coins and all will be well. You'll see," she patted his shoulder before gathering up an armload of books.

As Pliny idly wondered if his sister kept some coins on her for just such an occasion, he mulled over his findings. There seemed to be no evidence that Jupiter and the Imperial Pantheon had ever truly existed on Old Terra, it was a matter of simple faith.

But, what was faith? Was he expected to humbly embrace his new life, or was his rebirth a chance for a new meaning, a chance to eke out a life serving a higher calling? One that held sway over others.

Pliny stood and made his way out of the library, ignoring the sidelong glare of a small woman in the cubicle next to him. He took in the grandeur of the building once again. Wooden pillars supported the many levels of books. The floor was white limestone tiles, patterned into the image of scrolls and books.

The intoxicating smell of old paper hung in the air. He resisted the urge to order down an old book just to smell it. Few people were present, likely because most popular information could be had for free on the Minerva network. Why go to the library when Minerva provided all the Pantheon said they needed?

Pliny looked over his shoulder as he exited the library, happy to be back among the living. It was midday on this sunny weekend, and people were out in force. Bobbing heads of every color passed him as he left the imposing cathedral of the library. The roadways were also busy, making Pliny glad that he had elected to walk, rather than drive. Dust blew into his eyes as the breeze danced in his hair. Grit built up between his fingers and toes. For a moment he longed to be on the seaside, rather than the city center. But, he had to work tomorrow and there was much left for him to think about.

There was a market just down the street, where merchants hawked their wares. Pliny resisted the reflex to run far away, in fear of becoming a statistic yet again. One trip to Pluto's realm, or the Singularity, was enough for his lifetime. However, he had a great idea for a gift for his sister. She'd appreciate a life sized statue of Venus, wouldn't she?

Chuckling, he headed toward the market, steeling himself to the task of once again entering a crowd. He hoped he wouldn't get shot this time, as he'd neglected to make a backup of his brain after he left the library.

Chapter 10

Pliny sat at his dining room table, an ebony behemoth with six matching chairs. He'd taken down all of his iconic religious paintings and stowed them in the closet with his black toga, opting instead for the simplicity of bare walls. The empty space seemed a necessity while he figured out what had happened to him when he had almost died. Bare walls were not judgmental, nor were they reminiscent of his experience at the Market. Its blank space in his memory was unsettling, like a gap in his life. That gap had been filled by the Singularity.

Before him lying on the table was a noose tied with blue climbing rope. He'd looked up the directions for tying it on Minerva, hoping for the clarity which seemed only possible through death. Much like Roma IV, it was uniform, orderly. He ran his fingers along every fiber, along the creases at every joint in the knot. He counted the coils, tested the strength of the knot and the rope. He examined himself, taking note of his mental state. What was he really wanting to gain out of this experiment? Would this path give him what he truly wanted? Could he see the Singularity again? Should he? Maybe he was dead already and this was one of Pluto's clever ruses. Was he simply depressed, like his sister would say?

Pliny sighed, standing up and feeling the circulation rushing back to his legs. How long he had been sitting there, he didn't know. Pushing the dark thoughts from his mind, he decided to call his sister. She may not be the most supportive person around, but talking was supposed to help, or so common knowledge suggested. He smirked. With a personality like hers, it was no wonder she'd elected to work in the pharmaceutical industry.

He moved into his living room, the white walls reflecting the shimmering light of the holo-display. He willed the interface to life as he descended into his comfortable recliner, enjoying the comfort as a welcome relief from the hard ebony dining room chair. He commanded the machine to contact his sister, and waited for her to respond.

The image flickered in the middle of the room, replaced by Claudia's face, contorted into a frown. "Oh, it's you, *again*, big brother," she said.

Pliny rolled his eyes. "Who else calls," he asked.

"Oh, only about a hundred other people. I, you see, have friends. I bet you haven't even been to a party this decade."

"You'd be surprised," he said, shaking his head. He suppressed a smile. The less she knew about his intellectual explorations, the better.

"I'm sure you wanted to talk to me about something other than your usual attempts at banter."

"I'm in a bit of a hard spot," he began, rubbing his forehead. "I've been having a lot of doubts about life and my place in the world, and I need a rock."

"Okay, just call me 'Rocky.'"

"All right, Rocky, if that is your real name, I'm struggling with what happened to me at the Market," he said, holding his hands in his lap.

"That, again? You were snatched from the hands of Pluto and you can't even be grateful?" she rolled her eyes.

"It's not about gratitude, *Rocky*, it's about picking up the pieces and moving forward with my life despite what I saw."

"Maybe see a therapist? A priest of Pluto? Get laid? Try those, in some combination."

"Getting laid is nice, and I already talked to a priest. Therapy could help, or not. This thing, whatever it is, might not even be within the purview of standard psychology."

"Oh, come on. People have been restored from worse injuries than yours, and they're coping somehow. You probably couldn't even define psychology if you tried."

"But, do I still have a soul? Can they regrow that?" Pliny asked. "And I do know what psychology is, I took a class on it in college."

"Yeah, whatever. The better question would be where the soul of your apartment went. You had your walls covered in idols, now they're bare," she said, narrowing her eyes to slits.

"I'm just redecorating, so what?"

"You know it's bad luck to have bare walls."

"Says who?" he sighed.

"Oh, I don't know, maybe the whole Pantheon? Do you want them coming to do an intervention?"

Pliny suppressed a shudder. "Come on, it's not as though bare walls is a crime. I still have all the images; I just want to coordinate them with my furniture. The bust of Venus totally clutters up the dining room, if you know what I mean."

"No, but that's not unusual. You are a strange one, Pliny, always have been," she said. "Now, unless you're in pressing need of dying, I'm off to watch whatever is on the Minerva Enlightenment network. Goodnight, brother."

The display winked out, and Pliny palmed his face. What was he thinking, calling Claudia for help and understanding on a public channel? That kind of blatant blasphemy could get him a trip to the Imperial Pantheon's headquarters. *Snatched off the street in the wink of an eye,* he thought.

He switched the channel to Minerva Colosseum, anything to empty his mind. A man with a net and spear faced down against a man with a sword and small circular red shield. However, the darkness he felt inside him persisted despite his rising blood lust, and that damned noose remained foremost in his thoughts. Should he try to go back to the Singularity, or was his place here, on Roma IV? He had no idea how to reconcile the question of the soul, nor could he ask a priest, who would only give him answers that meant nothing. Pliny held onto hope that his predicament would simply fade away and he could go back to his boring job and his bachelor life.

He sat up, in sudden realization, eyes jerking away from the mindless combat of the beefy gladiators. He would talk to Tetra, and maybe she could supply answers to his questions. He would even cook for her, a pleasurable pastime which was his key card to second or third dates. He brought up her information on the holo-display, smiling as he made the call. Maybe his sister had actually helped, by simply being her usual unsympathetic self.

Chapter 11

Stir-fry was on the menu, and Pliny was standing at the kitchen counter chopping carrots when the doorbell buzzed. Tetra was right on time, he noted with a smile. He so hated the pathologically late; he saw it as the epitome of rudeness. He willed the door camera to display above the dining room table and admitted her almost immediately. His heart quickened as she climbed the stairs, her sandals pattering all the way up against the concrete floor. She knocked at his apartment's door.

"Come in," he answered, not missing a beat with his chopping.

Tetra stepped inside, and he took a moment to appreciate her knee-length lacy red dress and her signature streaked red and black hair. "Welcome," he said, offering a small bow.

She pulled a bottle of wine from her bag. "*In vino, veritas,*" she said with a wink. "A quote attributed to Pliny the Elder. I saw no reason for such a good saying to go to waste. In Latin, even. Better yet, you're also named Pliny. Must be why I like you."

"Only the best of truth for us," he replied. "And, I am Pliny the Best, I'm not self-identifying by age, yet."

"Pluto strike you down should you begin before the age of

120. Nice place, by the way," she said, looking into his living room. "Walls are a little bare, though. Not an icon kind of guy?"

"Not really, I just needed quieter surroundings to think," he replied.

"Thinking … I can appreciate a good think," she said as she approached the counter. "Sometimes, I brew a pot of coffee and just sit down with my thoughts." She took another glance into the living room. "You have a mental backup unit? Sweet!"

"Can't afford to lose all of those important thoughts and memories," he said, laughing. "Rest assured, it's running on continuous backup. I won't miss a thing."

"Good, I want you to remember every salacious moment."

Pliny dumped the carrots into the wok and turned up the heat. "I hope you like stir-fry. I have very good success with this dish."

"I'll eat almost anything, don't worry about me," she said. "How about some wine? I brought the Bacchus Special Reserve, the kind from the grocery store!"

"Excellent choice in wine, but will you eat even your words?"

"Especially those."

Pliny smiled. This was going to be a good night.

***

Pliny's head tingled from the continuous mental backups being run as he sipped his glass of wine. They were sitting on the large sofa in the living room. The alcohol had begun to work its magic, and his thoughts were running more freely—as was his tongue.

"I was dead once, you know," he said. Now was as good a time as any to present his suppositions.

Tetra sat up straight. "They brought you back? How did you die?"

I was hit by a kinetic rifle bullet at the Saturnalia Market a few weeks ago. The injury was really bad, destroyed most of my brain. But, thanks to the backup unit, they were able to rebuild my brain and skull," he said.

"You were there at the market? Your restoration, it seems so perfect. They barely managed to put my colleague back together after her accident," she said, looking into her glass of wine. "She never taught again… but, you were saying?"

"There's more… that you might be able to help me with." Pliny swirled the wine glass, watching the red liquid move with the motion. Despite being cheap, the wine's vineyard predated the rule of Nero II two thousand years before, and the vintage was rooted deep in the world's history.

"How could an esoteric academic like myself help with a real-world problem?" she said, giggling. Her cheeks were flushed.

"It's in your area of expertise. I saw something while I was dead, and I can't figure out what it was, or what the meaning of it was," he replied.

"Now, that's juicy. You gotta tell me."

"It was a circular void, almost like a reversed lens. Stars warped around the edge of it, and fire erupted from its poles. I think I saw the singularity, not Pluto's realm."

"Sounds like you saw a black hole," she said, taking a sip. "You're right, this is good."

"The wine or the story?"

"Both," she said with a smile.

He hummed as he took another sip of wine. "But, what does it all mean? I know I was dead, but what do you see after you die? There are no resources available to the public that explain death, and books on cosmology are heavily guarded by the librarian."

"I feel like you're trying to ask me something," she said, raising an eyebrow.

"Maybe a small favor," he said, lowering his voice to a playful whisper. "It shouldn't be a problem for someone of your learning."

"Well, spit it out. We don't have all night for pleasantries," she arched an eyebrow.

"All I want is a little peek at some journals of a philosophical nature. They're not cheap, and I'd need to justify why I want them to the Investigations Board. Do you have access?"

"Of course I do, but I have to know, why is this investigation so important to you?" she asked.

"I need to know what I saw. I need to know," he said, trailing off.

"Know what?"

"If I still have a soul."

Tetra opened her mouth, and quickly closed it. "An excellent question," she replied.

"If not for me, then out of professional curiosity?"

"Right, as fodder for my next paper, perhaps?" she said, giggling. "I can't even imagine justifying that subject to the Pantheon's approval board."

"You have to start sometime," Pliny said, raising his glass.

She toasted him. "You're lucky you're cute."

Pliny laughed.

Chapter 12

Pliny sat in the cafeteria lunchroom, an insignificant speck, sandwiched within the high ceiling and endless white walls. Harsh lighting glared overhead, causing him to squint as he slurped his hot soup. Across from him sat Felix, his colleague.

"Slurp louder, I don't think they heard you back in the lab," Felix said.

Pliny shrugged and took a dainty spoonful, instead.

"You're doing this just to annoy me, like how you won't tell me what death feels like." Felix knit his brow and shook his head.

"Okay, fine, I'm working on the proper way to present it to you, maybe in crayon," Pliny said.

Felix groaned. "You told me that after our evening out at the wine bar a few weeks ago. You need to give me more. Don't leave me hanging like this. Maybe I can help."

"Help, what kind of help?" Pliny looked down at his soup and regretted not eating at his desk.

"My sister is a psychologist, and a good one too. If you need to heal, I can make the introduction. I'm good like that," Felix replied.

"I'm not sure if I'm looking for that level of commitment."

"Just saying, you seem a little… gloomy lately," Felix said. "I'm totally your guy if you need to work things out. I get it, and I'm buying a brain backup unit thingy you'll be happy to know."

"At least my life is serving as a cautionary tale. Okay, fine. I'll spill it. But not here in the open, I would prefer to keep my existential crisis private, if you know what I mean," Pliny said.

"My lips are sealed, but everyone here already knows your angsty origin story you know."

"But you have to do something for me, too," Pliny said, lowering his voice.

Felix put his hands on the table, rattling its uneven legs, causing Pliny's soup to slosh. "Let's hear it," Felix said.

"You need to hear me out on what I think I really saw. I'm working on a theory and I need an opinion from a passionate and curious layman."

"I can do this. Your place or mine this time?"

"Yours," Pliny said, stirring his soup. "You bring the wine," he concluded.

"Deal."

***

Pliny and Felix stood in front of Felix's modest apartment building in a poorer part of town, a low brick structure with large windows and wrought iron balconies. A retinal scanner was affixed next to the lock on the building's red entry door. The cool breeze from the sea tickled Pliny's skin, sending an army of goosebumps rushing up his arms. His plain green tunic did little to protect him from the chilliness of the dying day.

Felix was digging in his brown canvas bag, looking for his keys. Pliny hoped Felix wouldn't drop the wine, which was of a decent vintage from a vineyard on the other side of the Nostrum sea. A key was eventually produced, and the door unlocked with the combination of his key and the retinal scanner. A warm gust of air greeted Pliny, as well as the rich aroma of roasting lamb. "What's for dinner?" he asked.

"Not lamb, unfortunately. I figured we could order something from Aurora's. Do you like their food?"

"Love it, sure. Why not indulge? We're only confronting my mortality. Can't do that on an empty stomach." Pliny laughed.

"Exactly," Felix said, ushering Pliny along a narrow corridor marked with scuffs and scrapes to a set of stairs at the end. "We're going to the third floor. Hope you keep up with leg day."

"Everyday is leg day when you live in one of these buildings," Pliny said. "Don't you make enough to move to a better building?"

They entered the stairwell, and it was just as narrow and ill-lit as the hallways. Felix took the lead, leaving Pliny to navigate the stairs in hot pursuit. He was made grateful that his own building had only one set of stairs. "There's no elevator? That's not very accessible."

"Us stone-age barbarians gotta live somewhere," Felix said.

They reached the top, ascending to the peak height of the stairs. Felix had his keys out. They stopped in front of unit 314, where Felix inserted his key and pressed his face to the retinal scanner. The door slid open, and Felix gestured Pliny inside. "Welcome to my humble home, don't mind the mess," Felix said.

Pliny stepped inside the small apartment. The air was stale and the interior slightly cluttered. A gray leather sofa dominated the left wall, and a holo-display had been installed in the center of the room. To the right was a small kitchen and a set of closed doors lead to what Pliny figured was the bedroom and bathroom. "It's not so bad, what do you mean by cluttered?"

Felix laughed. "I knew I liked you for a reason, and it's not even related to the dead-ness. Take a seat.”

Pliny walked over to the sofa and moved some papers before sitting down. He sank into what he affectionately referred to as a bum-eating couch. “Nice seat,” he said.

Felix came to join him, two wine glasses in hand. “Now, you’re going to reveal all your secrets to me, whether you want to or not. The power of wine compels you! Just, not the kind of secrets that will get me yanked. My brother in-law’s cousin vanished recently.” Felix lowered his voice. “It may have been the Inquisitors, his name was Claudius. Good guy.”

Pliny frowned. “I’m sorry to hear of that, I shall say a prayer to Jupiter for Claudius’ safe return before I sleep. Now, I’ve held up my end of the bargain, so hit me with your best shot.”

“Thank you, Pliny. Jupiter will make it all right, the man was no heretic. On to happier subjects, so tell me everything,” Felix said, his distant gaze returning to the world.

“Okay. Being dead was kind of strange. It’s almost like nothing happened. I remember the end of my last mental backup, but nothing from the Saturnalia market, as I’m sure you’d expect.”

Felix nodded. “And what comes next?”

“Before I woke up in the hospital, I saw this black body encircled by a halo of distorted stars, with red jets erupting from the poles. It was surreal, beyond anything I had ever imagined.”

“Did you see the river? Was it a kind of door? Where was the boatman?”

“Nothing at all like that. I suppose that the infinite darkness of that spot could have been a portal, or something beyond normal human experience. It seemed to spin, and the lights turned in on themselves. No boatman or river Styx, though.”

Felix cupped a hand over his mouth. “Then what does all that mean?”

“That’s just it, I’ve been hunting for answers for the past few weeks and nothing helps."

"Did you talk to a priest?" Felix asked.

"I went to Pluto's temple first, they just said that I saw the gates to Pluto's Realm and that I had been blessed."

"What do *you* think you saw?" Felix asked.

"Do you watch Minerva Enlightenment?" Pliny asked.

"All the time, I love that channel."

"Did you see their special documentary on black holes a few weeks ago?" Pliny took a sip of wine after asking the question.

"That was awesome, I loved that one. Do you think you saw a black hole?"

"I've been doing research in the library on my own time, and it makes sense. Maybe my soul was sucked into the singularity while I was being reconstructed?" Pliny took a large gulp of wine this time. Even admitting his thoughts required fortification.

"Whoa, did you just say you lost your soul?"

Pliny shrugged. "It's possible, if souls are indeed real."

Felix hushed him. "Don't say that too loudly. Claudius made that joke once last Saturnalia."

Pliny nodded and sipped his wine.

"You want to know what I think?" Felix asked, a grin returning to his face.

"What is it?"

"I think you did see something. Maybe you were crossing into the event horizon of a black hole. Damn things need to exist for a reason, right? Maybe they're the key to it all!" Felix looked as though he'd discovered the theory of everything in that very moment, eyes wide and excited.

"I'm not sure that's how astrophysics works," Pliny replied.

"Hear me out, Pliny, what you saw looked exactly like that black hole on Minerva, right?"

Pliny nodded.

"So, let's assume you really were on the verge of getting

sucked into an infinite singularity. That tips over almost everything we've learned since birth, you follow?"

"So, what does this have to do with my soul? I'm still me!"

"What I'm getting to is that maybe you have work to do, even though the physical damage was completely repaired. You need to heal your mind." Felix hushed his voice and looked to the locked door.

"Enlighten me already. You sound like my sister."

"You need a vacation, and to get a few orbits around the nearest black hole. Take control of your life. Own your death and start this fresh life off on the right foot," Felix said.

"A black hole cruise? Those are prohibitively expensive! I don't have two weeks off right now."

"You can work it, seriously. Just talk to the boss, he probably wants to stop paying you for a week or two anyway. Use your damn bonus on it instead of painting your walls white. Again."

"Yes, I could do that," Pliny sighed. His walls were getting tarnished and he needed to fill the holes from where his idols used to hang.

"Just think of it, and you can tell me more about your death."

Pliny swirled his wine. "That's all I'm going to say."

Chapter 13

"Go on a cruise, with you? Are *you* insane?" Claudia's face was suspended from the ceiling of Pliny's apartment, the harsh light glaring off his still pictureless white walls. Pliny sat in his recliner, hands on his lap. His eyes ached from another day at work, staring at those damned picobots, and he badly needed a nap. But instead he found himself seeking out a traveling partner for his pilgrimage to see a black hole.

"Why not? You could at least be supportive of my second-life crisis," Pliny said, forcing a chuckle.

"What I'm not supportive of is you getting all of these crazy, blasphemous ideas and trying to cover it up as some bizarre, life-changing event that everyone in your life gets exposed to." Claudia's fake blond curls bounced as she shook her head. She wiped one eye with the back of her hand. "I have to look over my shoulder every time I go out because of what you tell me! You must accept reality and the Gods before it's too late!"

"This is my life. And this is important to me, is it so bad to want to share part of my personal growth and struggle with the one family member I have left? The Pantheon doesn't care, they'd have pulled me by now if they did." Pliny said.

"You are impossible. Take a friend, or something. If people

were meant to go to black holes, we wouldn't have to need special ships to avoid the time side-effects, to name just one good reason. Another is that everything you need to heal is embracing the Gods."

Pliny sighed. "Okay, fine, forget I said anything."

"Already forgotten, brother. Now, if you'll excuse me, I have a date."

"Another?"

"Yes, you should try it sometime, you might actually like it," she said, with an even sharper edge to her voice.

"Have fun," Pliny said, before willing the screen to close. He sat with his thoughts a while, ruminating over their exchange. He rubbed his forehead. Was he blasphemous? Both Felix and Claudia had expressed their doubts about his suppositions, and their ideas for the cause of his death-experience were drastically different. Could he find a middle ground, somewhere that reconciled his experiences with natural law and theological truths?

He pushed himself out of his comfortable seat and paced the length of the room. He ground his teeth, clenching enough to tense the muscles in his temples. He considered a run to the library to clear his head, but curfew was already in effect. Perhaps Felix or Tetra would go with him on his cruise, for novelty's sake. The notion of going with Tetra was definitely appealing. Beautiful and intelligent, she was so unlike most everyone he'd had the pleasure of conversing with. But, would she accept, and more importantly, would she support his theories?

Perhaps there was another option. He could contact Gaius, a man he'd met at a discussion group and hadn't recontacted since their meeting weeks ago. Pliny willed the man's contact information onto the screen and sought out a painkiller for his headache.

He returned to the living room and cozied up to his perch in his recliner, his headache already receding to a dull throb. The connection began, and Gaius's face flickered to life below the projector.

"Pliny, I thought I'd never hear from you again," the man said, a wide smile glowing on his face.

"It's been a tough week, but I was wondering if we could make time to talk. I've been doing some research and a whole lot of thinking. I really believe I'm onto something and could use a fresh perspective."

"Anything you need, I can't get enough intelligent conversation."

"Meet me at Aurora's tomorrow after work?"

"See you there."

***

Aurora's was bustling as always—the small upscale pub was filled to the brim with people, all young and well-dressed. The decor was wood, and the walls were lined with wine bottles. Mirrors with the logos from a variety of vineyards emblazoned on them graced the walls. The smell of frying food infused the air. The lighting was turned down. It was just bright enough to read the menu and the expression on Gaius' face. They were seated in the back, towards the kitchen and toilets. An unenviable position, but it would have to do. A young couple sat next to them, holding hands on the table and with their other hands alternated sipping from glasses of red wine and picking away at a plate of fried Roma dodo wings. Pliny considered ordering some for himself, it was an acceptable treat.

As they got comfortable, a waitress came with a wine list and menu. Pliny ordered the house wine, while Gaius opted for some obscure re-opened vineyard that Pliny had never heard of. Vinea Zimmer, it was called. Pliny wondered at the name—Zimmer wasn't proper. How did it get past the censors?

"So, Pliny, what can I do for you? Gaius asked, as he leafed through the food menu.

Pliny stopped mulling over the names of wines. "I have a theory on what happened to me when I died, but I need unbiased feedback."

"Out with it," Gaius said.

"I think I saw a black hole while my brain was being reconstructed."

"You sure do need that unbiased opinion. What does that even mean?" Gaius put down his wine and pressed his index finger on the menu to make some selections.

"I think I saw the gate to somewhere, but I was snatched away before I passed through. I need to know if it's real. I think I know how to prove it, though."

"How so?"

"I think I need to take a black hole cruise, see it with my own eyes. It's preferable to dying again," Pliny said, with a smirk.

"That's for sure," Gaius said, stroking his chin.

"What say you?"

"Should I be worried you're a suicide risk?" Gaius arched an eyebrow.

"No, nothing like that. Maybe I'll just burn some vacation days and get this nagging uncertainty over with."

"You know what, I could get you that cruise at a reduced rate. My brother owns a travel agency, and they plan these trips all the time, they're that popular. Why is beyond me." Gaius shrugged.

Pliny sat upright in his chair. "Sign me up, I just need to know if what I saw is real."

Gaius laughed and put his forearm on the table. A shimmering green-red holographic projection winked into existence, with a short memo being written at the speed of thought. "There we go, I'll probably hear back in a day or two. Good?"

Pliny nodded and took a sip of his wine. His thoughts raced—could he really take this trip on his own without expending his life savings? Better yet, would it bring clarity?

"Say, Pliny, have you ever ridden in a small suborbital craft before?" Gaius asked.

"No, why?" Pliny asked.

"I'm working on getting my license. I need to log some hours, and sometimes it gets boring up there. How about you come along and we can talk philosophy away from prying ears? What do you say?"

Pliny smiled. "Sign me up, just don't get me killed."

"No promises."

As they chatted about mundane matters and sipped their wine, neither of them noticed the demure woman in a black dress sitting alone at the table behind them.

Chapter 14

Aelia fumed as she paced her tiny apartment, kicking a wooden chair into the corner, far out of her way. The holo-display was off, and the dying day cast long shadows into the room. Why was Pliny so fascinating? Why hadn't she brought him in and put him to the question? She'd busted people for less. She wanted to return home, tour the temple of the Imperial Pantheon and receive a proper reward for her service. But, what did she have? Libraries, philosophical conventions, even a visit to the obsidian temple of Pluto. Even the recently booked black hole cruise wasn't strong evidence of blasphemy.

But, what was blasphemy? Was it a thought to be self-censored? Was it a seditious lie to cover up a lack of faith in the natural order of things? Worse, could it be contagious? The more she skimmed Pliny's activities, the more she wanted to connect with him and truly understand such an obvious personal awakening. Could she be guilty of a similar heresy for allowing his activities to continue, and letting him affect her?

No, her loyalties were rigid and unyielding. She'd broken humans into babbling husks in the name of Jupiter and scoured out rat's nests of impurity with the wrath of Juno. What God would inspire her with Pliny? She'd seen the man several times.

He had bumped into her as he was leaving the philosophical conference. What stayed her hand, she didn't know. The babble of a philosopher was barely tolerated, and far-flung notions of the oneness of humanity were simply absurd. Could that be the key? Then she'd tailed him to a library, where she'd commanded the librarian to reveal his reading list. She'd even dined alone at some tavern. She longed to be home, with her sisters in the dormitory.

Aelia stopped in her tracks, placing both palms on the flimsy kitchen table. She needed to actually talk to Pliny, without him knowing that she was an Inquisitor. Honey before vinegar, so to speak.

Aelia straightened as another thought struck her. She needed to get close to him, that she knew. She moved to the shabby couch and commanded the holo-interface to come to life. The small room lit up like a flash of fire. She willed the connection to her matron, Marcia. When the screen activated the other woman's scowl twisted into an abortive attempt at a smile. "Yes, child?"

Aelia swallowed before beginning, "Mistress, I believe I've found a way to infiltrate Pliny Augur and his followers."

"How so?"

"He is going to take a black hole cruise, a pilgrimage of sorts. I want to be on that ship. To befriend him and learn the depth and breadth of his unholy slander. It is not enough that the organizer of the conference witnessed him, nor his development of new associations," Aelia said, folding her hands onto her lap. "I am so close. But, I need to get conclusive proof of any contamination he's caused. This could be big, it could even be big enough for a purge."

"A purge? I see, and I expect you'll need funding for that voyage, correct?" The Mistress frowned.

"Yes, Mistress." She bowed her head.

Marcia sighed. "Very well, you may take this trip, but I expect results."

"Thank you." Aelia bowed her head in reverence.

The video feed winked out, and Aelia turned to her computer. She checked her available funds and was pleased to see that the necessary amount had already been deposited into her expense account. She arranged to be booked on the same cruise as him with her Imperial authorization, before turning her attention back to reviewing Pliny's mental notes. It was a tedious job, but she needed to know what it was she was up against. Was it only him, or were there other conspirators as well?

But, part of her groaned. She didn't want to see a black hole. The notion of such a thing was unsettling, and an affront to all she considered coherent and orderly in the universe. She bowed her head and cupped hands in her lap. "Jupiter hear me, Juno give me strength, Minerva grant me boundless wisdom…" she intoned, beginning the devotion that so often gave her clarity. None came.

Chapter 15

It was a crisp, bright morning in the calm month after the Saturnalia frenzy, and the massive orb-shaped cruise ships leaving the planet were a near constant sight to behold in the sunrise. The hum and roar of anti-grav engines reverberated in Pliny's chest, and his stomach turned in on it. He'd never been off-world before, and a month or two ago he would have never expected that he'd feel the desire to take a trip to the stars. He considered himself at most a beach-goer when it came to trips. This particular cruise ship was a gray monstrosity resembling an elongated cylinder but with a blunted nose and small wings. It sat upright on the launch pad, its nose prepared to part the heavens in a roar of glory. Along its side was the ship's name: *Void Star*.

Pliny's hands balled into fists as the departure time was announced. He didn't like the notion of space travel, but here he was, on a mission for personal knowledge and spiritual satisfaction. A small woman with fine features and long brown hair stood next to him, gazing at the same ship. Pliny thought she looked familiar, but from where he didn't know. It's possible she'd attended one of the same parties or conferences as him, or perhaps just a face in the thousands that paraded past him on any given day on the way to work or the market.

She turned to him. "Have you been off-world before?" she asked.

"Never, this is kind of a one-time deal," Pliny replied. "How about you?"

"The same. Wanted to do this since I was a young girl, just never had the chance before. This truly is the chance of a lifetime for me," she replied.

"I hope this trip is worth the money, I've heard good reviews though. Who did you book with?" he asked.

"Only the best from Mercury Travels," she said, winking.

"As long as we don't come back 500 years in the future, that is," Pliny said, laughing.

"Come on, like that's ever happened." She crossed her arms.

"Just once, during an early expedition."

"You've done your homework, how reassuring!" The woman rolled her eyes and looked back at the *Void Star*.

"Well, I don't want it to end up being a one-way trip. My sister would come back from the grave and kill me."

A beep sounded, cutting the air with a metallic voice. "All passengers for the *Void Star* please proceed to docking port Omicron-five."

"I guess that's our queue. Are you traveling alone?" Pliny asked.

"I was supposed to go with a friend, but she chickened out at the last minute. But now, I've just met someone to talk to on the way." She extended a hand. "Aelia, at your service."

Pliny took her hand. "Pliny Augur, pleased to meet you. Shall we?"

***

Pliny sat in his chair, pondering his life choices. His stomach twisted even tighter as they waited for countdown, a large viewscreen suspended on the wall ahead. Aelia had arranged to get her seat moved closer to him, which was a welcome distraction while sitting in the large room designed for lift-off and landing. The space was the size of a coliseum field, with passengers as far as he could see. Men, women, even children were lined up for the trip of a lifetime. *Better this than another death*, Pliny thought, thinking of the still-tied noose hanging in his closet. He clenched his fist on the arm of his chair, and tapped the soft fabric in time with his breaths. He closed his eyes. Just a few moments of terror before he could duck inside of his quarters and calm down.

The countdown began. Pliny held his breath, as each syllable echoed in his ears. *No no*, he thought. But he was committed, locked in to this adventure, and there was no turning back. Pressure built in his chest and he exhaled slowly.

When the world erupted into a quaking cacophony, Pliny's eyes flew open. The reverberations of the engines filled his chest, forcing him to inhale sharply. His seat groaned as the rumbling continued, the vista projected on the screen ahead seemed nothing more than a white barricade. As the cloud approached, Pliny wondered what the great void would be like. Would this become a more peaceful trip once out in space, or would the engine noises always predominate? He supposed that should have been a question for the travel agency.

In an instant, the wispy clouds parted, exposing a rich star-studded vista beyond anything he'd seen on *Minerva*, or out star-gazing while camping. Constellations usually obscured by city lights were there in plain view, their stars burning with nuclear fusion that was no longer obscured by the atmosphere. Pliny's eyes traced every shape and line, finding familiar friends and new fascinations. The twin moons hung overhead, a reminder of where he was. *Goodbye, Roma IV*, he thought.

Aelia looked his way. "That wasn't so bad," she said, pressing her lips together. She was pale.

"I think I left my heart back on the spaceport," he said.

"I'm going to straighten up and get settled in my cabin. Meet me for dinner?" she asked.

"Sure, I'd like that. Do you like pub food?"

"Love it," she replied.

Chapter 16

Pliny sat at a table in one of the ship's onboard restaurants, taking in the view and the incredibly expensive wine list. Some glasses alone were a day's wages for him. He suppressed a shudder as he considered opting for a cheaper beer instead. The huge room that was located on the upper deck had a panoramic view of the stars. Padded metal chairs were set at every table, and the lights were muted. The ambiance was crowded, but cheerful. A few squeals of delighted children filtered down from the family restaurant upstairs, but that was easily ignored. Pliny sat back in his chair, his hands clammy in his lap. His stomach fluttered, but not from hunger. He didn't know why, as dates were usually effortless for him. Aelia must be different, somehow, in a way he couldn't place yet.

Aelia approached from the staircase and paused for a moment, her eyes darting from table to table. There was something about her, almost feline in grace. Pliny raised his hand to wave her over. She drifted towards him, her red dress moving over the curves of her body. The sight left him intoxicated and he revisited the idea of sharing a bottle of wine with her.

"Hi Aelia," Pliny began, offering her the seat across from him. "You look lovely."

Aelia laughed and blushed. "I hoped you'd like it," she replied.

"What's not to like? Have a seat, let's get some wine and get to know each other," Pliny said, passing her the wine list.

"By Juno, these are some expensive wines! What happened to plain old house wine?"

"That's the cruise lifestyle, I guess. Run up the tab for a captive audience. Do you like Zimmer?" he asked, putting his latest discovery to the test.

"I love Zimmer," Aelia replied.

Pliny flagged a waitress with a long brown braid wearing a short skirt and a white buttoned up shirt. She appeared by their side in a shimmer of light. *A holographic server, how interesting*, he thought.

"What can I get for you?" the holo-server asked.

"A bottle of Zimmer 4007, and a platter of finger foods, please," Pliny said.

"Right away," the server said, vanishing from their side back to her post in the center of the room.

In an instant, the bottle and wine glasses were produced by a flesh-and-blood staff member wearing a black dress, and Pliny poured for them. He raised his glass to toast: "To new encounters."

She smiled and returned the toast. "I hope that our conversations will prove to be both fruitful and enlightening," she replied, casting him a wolfish grin.

Pliny laughed, wondering how he'd been so fortunate to have this beautiful woman's attention. It seemed their encounter was a random, and pleasant experience.

"So, tell me about yourself," Aelia said, taking a sip of wine. She smiled.

"Not too much to tell. I'm a picotech assembler and I live in the Caesarea district in the Sacred City. I have an annoying little sister and I spend too much time watching Minerva.”

“Picotech, that must be hard on the eyes,” she said.

“You get used to it. The worst part of it is the stress.” Pliny took a sip of wine, moving it around in his mouth to get the full effect of the subtle flavors. The dryness washed over his taste buds and he smiled. “You have to mind the gray goo, but not think too hard about the implications of the stuff.”

Aelia leaned in, plucking a Roma dodo wing off of the platter. “Gray goo?” she asked.

“It’s a kind of man-made disaster in which runaway picobots begin to reproduce out of control,” he said.

“That’s terrifying! How in Jupiter’s name do you stay calm enough to function?”

“Well… the pay helps, but in reality we can stop them using temperature. Flash them down to absolute zero and then disassemble them with our tools.”

“Has that ever happened to you?”

“Just once, on my first week out of training. It was terrifying. Thank Jupiter Felix was there to help me through it, or Roma IV might be a mass of picobots floating in orbit.”

“Felix is your boss?” she asked.

“No, just a colleague, and a friend. This cruise was his idea, actually.”

“What a great friend to have, did he have any other ideas for you?”

“I stand by all of my friends, and that includes my little sister. And no, I seldom take Felix’s advice. He’s too young for that. Now, on to something more interesting. Tell me about yourself,” Pliny said.

“Not much to tell, I’m a human resources interviewer. I spend my days asking questions and trying to learn as much about a person as possible,” she said.

Pliny sat back. “Is this just another day on the job for you?”

"Not at all. I actually like you," she replied, twirling her braid. "Besides, it's good to take time off. As much as I enjoy asking people about their professional lives, I like actual connection with humans from time to time even more."

"An introverted questioner, who would have thought it possible?"

"Laugh all you like, I always find my mark." She folded her hands in front of her on the table, rubbing her fingers with a napkin.

"Am I your mark?" he asked, sniffing his wine.

"You are now."

Chapter 17

Aelia leaned against the railing. She was on the observation deck, and the dimly lit room was the perfect place to meditate on her encounter with Pliny. Stars raced by. The low hum of the engine was a welcome respite from the dull roar of the pub's incessant chatter. The buzz of the wine was still with her. The quiet room was ideal to reflect on her mission, and what she'd learned so far. On the surface, Pliny seemed innocent enough. He wasn't spewing his theories without prompting and seemed more interested in socializing with her than telling her about his brain reconstruction. She watched a large star zip by, which led to her next line of thought. *How will I justify this expense to the Mistress if I can't uncover anything damning?* she thought.

Maybe, she would need to make him implicate himself. She didn't have her usual tools—mental probes, imprisonment, or simple torture—but she did have his ear. Often, that was enough. Sometimes men fell apart before she even touched them, so why not stay civil while interrogating him? She'd done stranger things than romancing a miscreant, such as hallucination-induced scenarios designed to control what a suspect perceived, but she didn't know if the gambit would pay off. She dug her nails into her palms. She'd used the excuse of being tired to slip away from the pub, with the hopes of calming herself and allowing the complimentary brain backup device to commit her dinnertime experience into a cybernetic storage unit. She hoped that at least there could be some interesting material to present. But, perhaps she would skip the part about gray goo. It was unnerving and she could do without that kind of knowledge.

Even more troubling was the fact that she genuinely liked the man. Even his silly needless bald spot was endearing. He was easy to talk to, had a good job, and was everything she could want. But, the choice had to be duty above all-else. She still dreamed of a future of learning alongside Mistress Marcia, maybe even taking control of the Imperial Pantheon herself when the time was right. But for the moment, she would have to concentrate her efforts on Pliny.

***

Aelia sat in her comfortable cabin, leaning back against the gray sofa. She'd turned the lighting down in order to watch the passing of stars in peace and without distractions. The cabin was small and only had a small adjacent bathroom, but it was more comfortable than her Caesarean make-shift home, and far quieter than the dormitory room she'd shared with other Sisters of the Pantheon while she was in training. It was ten-by-ten paces long, with a large bed dominating the left corner of the room, and some dressers to its right. There was a small desk in the middle of the window, facing the stars. The back wall had a small gray two-seater sofa. She moved the desk's chair and took her shoes off, propping her feet on it for additional comfort as she sat on the sofa. She was not accustomed to fancy footwear, instead electing for sandals or simple athletic shoes.

She wiggled her toes as she turned the conversation over and over in her mind. This was the first time she'd lied during an assignment. She'd never used an assumed identity, or claimed to be a "human resources interviewer." She had, however, been truthful about Pliny being her mark. The situation was complicated, but she thought she could endure and press on. Infiltration wasn't her specialty, interrogation and the unpleasantness that went with it were.

She willed the holo-projector to life, the shimmering lights appearing to replace the starry vista of her windows. She checked the time at the Pantheon, and placed a call to Marcia.

The gray-haired woman's face emerged from the light, head cocked and frowning. "Status," she said.

"I have managed to befriend Pliny Augur," Aelia said.

"Do you have anything of substance?"

"Not yet, but I'm working on him. This is challenging without my usual equipment. Agony probes are far more reliable."

"I understand, however, you have ten days to extract a confession or a false positive. Is that understood?"

Aelia nodded and swallowed.

"Now, is there anything else you need?"

"Not at the moment, Mistress."

"Thank you for the update. Now, get back to work."

The screen winked out. Aelia did the one thing she knew would bring her clarity—she sat in the lotus position and meditated as the Pantheon had taught her. Deep breaths and intoning the names of the gods.

"Jupiter."

Breath.

"Juno."

Breath.

"Diana." The huntress. Perhaps the goddess Aelia would venerate in tonight's ritual. Her hunt was only just beginning, and her prey cunning. It would be a difficult chase.

Chapter 18

Pliny stood at the head of the observation deck, squinting into the distance. He'd woken early to avoid the crowds of parents and children hogging the coveted spot. Stars littered his peripheral vision, but his real target lay dead ahead. Somewhere, out there, lay the black hole he'd made the pilgrimage to see. Could the open wound inside his mind be repaired by simple proximity? Or would it take something much more extreme to reach his goal of understanding what had happened to him in that hospital room— like the noose in his closet, perhaps. Pliny shuddered, he didn't like the thought of it. He wasn't suicidal, rather, he quite enjoyed living, but he couldn't see himself continuing without answers to the question that mattered most: did he still have a soul? What was a soul, even? A metaphor for reaching the underworld and ultimate judgment? An animating spirit that runs through every living creature? Or, something artificial created to keep humans obedient? The last one was blasphemy, but Pliny reflected on it anyway. His mental records were confidential, after all. Nobody would care about some harmless philosophizing. It wasn't defying the gods' will, nor did it interfere with the teachings of the Imperial Pantheon.

As he mulled over what he was trying to see out in deep space, he sensed a movement behind him. Looking over his shoulder, it was Aelia who stood there, his new friend. He smiled. "Hello again," he said.

"Greetings to you, too," she giggled.

Pliny turned, bracing his back against the railing. "I was hoping you'd come back. I was just looking to see if we could view the black hole yet."

"Aren't you an eager one?" she asked.

"I have my reasons," Pliny said, looking over his shoulder.

"Do share."

"I'm just interested in the philosophical ramifications of a singularity. That's why I decided that the best course of action was to see one for myself," he replied, looking behind her as he spoke.

"So you're like a philosopher in your free time?" she folded her arms and cocked her head to the side.

"More or less. Gray goo hunting doesn't take much in the way of thinking once you get used to it."

"I see." Aelia said, smiling.

"Indeed. It's hard to find answers, as I'm sure you can imagine. Nobody knows, and neither do I."

"All too well. You never know what you're going to get," she said.

"What are you looking for out here?"

"A good time away from work. Being able to say I did it before I get too old, meet new people. Maybe pick up a souvenir or two for my friends."

"And here I am, only looking for my place in the universe."

"Is the goo factory not doing it for you?"

"Goo factory?" Pliny said, laughing. "No, just a few troubling things that happened to me that I can't shake. I figured I could do some soul-searching while on this trip and come back a new man."

"Want to pull up a chair and talk about it? I'm told I'm a very good listener. Maybe I can help," she said, gesturing towards a couch.

"Sure, why not." He moved towards the first row of couches. He sat down, and Aelia sat next to him, adjusting her skirt as she descended into the soft seat. "Wow, this couch is so spongy they'll need a crane to hoist me out of it!" he said.

"It sure is comfortable, though."

"This is crazy, I can't believe I met a stranger I can relate to," Pliny said, running a hand through his hair.

"Same here. I'm usually glued to the wall and hang out with the cat when I go to a friend's place. Now, where were we?"

"Talking about my deep thoughts," Pliny said.

"Yes, about that, don't keep me waiting," she said.

"It's not such a great story. Remember the terrorist attack on the Saturnalia market in the Caesarea district?" he asked.

"Yes, I remember, it was all over the news." She nodded.

"I took a bullet to the head and died. Long story short, I woke up in a hospital room with no idea what had happened to me, just a major headache and a hospital gown."

"What's so soul destroying about that? Your brain backup clearly worked out for you," she said.

"That's just it. I'm having the sinking suspicion that I left part of myself on that operating table, like a part of me died with my first brain."

"But, that's absurd. Your mind is reconstructed at the pico-level, there is no finer way to measure brain connectivity. And, unlike some, you clearly made it all the way back to the realm of the living." Aelia crossed her arms. "You're over thinking it."

"I know, but I need to see for myself. Look into the darkness and see if I am still whole," Pliny sighed.

"Why a black hole?"

"I saw something while they were reconstructing me, and I

can't explain it. I don't want to go into any further detail, but hopefully all will become clear when we get there and know more about the singularity."

"Right," she said, reaching out to take one of his hands into hers. "When you're ready, I'm here to listen. Dying must be quite the ordeal."

"I didn't care much for it," he said, taking her hand in his. It was soft and delicate. It felt right, somehow.

"Let's keep you on this side of Pluto's Realm, shall we?"

"I like the sound of that." Pliny smiled. "Now, breakfast?"

Chapter 19

Pliny wandered the front decks of the ship, breathing the recirculated air and walking in fake gravity. Even the progression of time was artificial—as time moved more slowly in proximity with large sources of gravity, they'd arrive back home far in the future without a source of artificial cadence. The ship had activated its negative-space drive, a device to keep them from losing Roma IV time to the singularity's gravity. He'd expected all of this and was eager to catch the first glimpse of his fixation, but the artificial feel was throwing off his response. The front deck faced the black hole. Pliny squinted to see if he could spot it, but all he saw were stars. Nothing giving off the appearance of a lens or accretion disk, nor were there any of the artifacts that could be seen in the x-ray spectrum. He wondered if he could request a live image in other bands of the electromagnetic spectrum. Perhaps, this could be an addition to his room.

Pliny left the forward deck and flagged down a host. His black suit and shirt devoured the light around him, and his black hair stood out starkly against the paleness of his face. "Excuse me, but is there any way to view the black hole through another spectrum?" he asked.

"Of course, we happily offer that service. I can have it patched through to your cabin for private viewing," the man said.

"Great, is there an extra charge for it?"

"Completely free, it's included in all of our travel packages but many people don't know to ask for it."

"Why wouldn't they?" Pliny was genuinely surprised. Why not enjoy the full extent of the cruise's luxuries?

"They come for the black hole, not to be unnerved by the swirling mass with jets blasting out of it. So we reserve that view for the people who want it." The man smiled as he spoke.

"Fair enough, can you patch it into room 455?"

The man lifted his arm, a small holo-display winking to life. With a few motions for his other hand the screen turned green and vanished. "Simply ask the computer to change spectra for you and enjoy the view," he said.

"Excellent, thank you for your help," Pliny said, turning to leave. He walked down the hall, humming.

As he stood by the elevator, a presence stirred behind him. "Hi!" the voice said.

Pliny turned around to the sound of the familiar voice. "Hi yourself," he said.

"Where are you off to? You're not doing your daily meditations out front?" Aelia asked.

"I had a new idea, so I'm heading back to my cabin to check out the black hole under some different spectra."

"What's that?" she asked.

"There are different ways to observe a black hole, through other kinds of electromagnetic spectra, and I was able to get my room's windows adjusted to view them. It's a feature that you have to ask for."

"Okay, I get it, I think." she wrinkled her nose.

"Come, join me. It will be fun to look at something other than stars."

"But, I like the stars. The Gods hung them there for a reason, right?" she said.

"Well, we can see more than stars. We did go on this cruise for a reason, too."

"So you keep reminding me," she said. "Why not. It's not like I'll get struck by lightning for looking at the singularity in a different way."

"And, hopefully, we'll keep a decent distance and not be sucked in."

"Remind me why I like you again?" she asked.

"It must be the bald spot," he replied, laughing.

***

Pliny peered into his cabin quickly, hoping to spot any mess or stray underwear before inviting Aelia in. The way was clear, so he ushered her inside and gestured to the sofa. "I'd offer you a drink, but there is no bar in my room," he said.

"The company will do nicely," she said, sinking into the couch. "I think your room is nicer than mine."

"I don't know how that's possible, I got one of the cheapest packages available," he said.

"We should go over the brochure for fun and profit, next time."

"So, there will be a next time?" Pliny asked.

Aelia laughed and slid closer to him. "I see potential." She winked.

Pliny inhaled deeply. Could this lovely woman have just been dropped into his life, in the aftermath of the shooting? It was a wonderful feeling, and warmth spread through his body. He wrapped his arm around her petite shoulders. "I'm not much of a traveler," he replied.

"Nobody's perfect," she said, laughing. "There are other ways to have fun."

"Like what?"

"Have you ever considered writing a book?" she asked.

"No, why do you ask?"

"Your experience at the market that day affected you, even I can see that. Writing always helps me set the story straight in my head and helps me heal when something bad happens. You should give it a go, maybe it will help you with your meditations," Aelia said, her eyes searching his face.

"I never thought of it like that. I haven't written anything since school. What would I even say? It'll all sound like the ramblings of a man barely able to keep his own story straight."

"It could always be non-fiction, or maybe even self-help. I'm sure lots of people with advanced cranial reconstructions have felt the same way. They need a lifeline. I can see how much the experience distressed you," she said.

"Yeah, I just want to go back to knowing what I believed, trusting my own senses and replacing my religious symbols in their spaces on my walls."

She gasped. "You took down your symbols?"

"Just for the moment. They were confusing me, and I needed breathing room."

"But the Gods are supposed to open our minds and our hearts! How could you abandon them like that?" she asked.

Pliny could feel her trembling under his arm. "Hey, it's okay, I'll just have my trip here, set things straight in my head and all will be as it should once again."

"But what about the Pantheon? What if they find out?" she asked.

"Well, let's just hope I get the right answers once this journey is over. I won't tell if you don't.

Aelia stood up, dabbing at her eyes.

"Aelia?"

"Not now, I need to think." She left the room without a word, leaving Pliny to stare at the stars, alone.

Chapter 20

Aelia was in tears when she reached her chamber, a narrow little nest that was easily half the size of Pliny's room. The bed was tiny and the holo-display dominated the ceiling, the star-field greeting her as it had before. She sank into the small loveseat, face in her hands. It was true, he'd actually committed the most blatant of blasphemies—rejecting the Gods in a time of need. A lapse in faith, even a small one, could delay the return of the Gods by hundreds of years. She'd sworn to protect them, given a sacred oath on her honor and her faith. How could she have been so blind, so malleable to discover that she had feelings for a heretic? But, she took some small consolation in the realization that if he did write down his thoughts, she'd have an airtight case to present to her Mistress.

She rubbed her eyes and sighed. This wonderful cruise, ruined by Pliny's admission of guilt. She couldn't stop thinking in terms of her and Pliny, what this would mean for them. As if they could even have a future. An Inquisitor and a heretic, only through Venus could they have a chance at a relationship. What kind of life was that? She refused to lie to herself and pretend that all was well. It didn't work like that, and she was too involved in her career—her dream—to leave it all for some man she'd been sent to investigate.

She ran her fingers through her hair, tugging at the scalp. She wished she was back home in the Imperial dormitory room she inhabited, without any concerns with respect to her duty and place in the universe. But, here she was. What was she to do when her heart called for Venus and her mind demanded to bring fourth Juno's spite?

The door buzzed, startling her. Was it time for the cleaners to do their work already? She stood up and walked to the door. She pressed the button to give admission, and there stood Pliny, with a bouquet of regal roses in hand. "Hey, I'm sorry I made you upset. Can we sit down and talk about how to make things right?" he asked.

"Okay," she said, rubbing her eyes. *Help me, Venus,* she thought. The impulse surprised her.

He walked into the room. "You've been crying," he said.

She nodded, stifling a sob with her hand.

Pliny came close, gathering her petite frame into his strong arms. He squeezed tight, making her warm and secure. "I never want to do anything to hurt you," he said.

She sniffled, wanting to be alone but desperately not wanting the moment to end. "But you did," she said.

"I'm so sorry. I want to make things right. Will you help me find my way again? Piousness is the way to honor the Gods, isn't it?"

"Yes, but—" she stammered.

"All can be forgiven if I take the proper path. The Gods are wise beings, they should be able to see the pure intentions in my heart," he said.

"Yes, I suppose they could. But how are they supposed to come back if we turn away from them?"

"I don't have a good answer to that. But, it was Nero II's commandment, and Vespasian VII will carry it through as it was originally commanded.”

“But you could be punished for even thinking otherwise!” she said.

“I doubt anyone will care about the eccentricities of one man with who was given a new chance at life. I just need to see this for myself and I can move on. You understand, don’t you? It’s just to set myself right, so I can go back to my meditations and devotions.”

“I guess,” she said, letting her head rest on his chest while the rose thorns prickled against her back.

“I feel like an idiot. I should never have put you in that position. I didn’t realize how important faith is to you. I can respect that, believing in something. Without a passion, life falls apart. My sister taught me that. You’d like her, and she’d love you.”

Aelia nodded, her tears drying but not enough to stop her accursed sniffling. She was stronger than this, how could she be so weak?

“Let’s go to the observation deck. No politics, no religion. Just you and I, enjoying the view. We can figure out the rest later,” Pliny said.

“Okay, but promise me one thing,” she said. She needed to go with him, though on a fundamental level she knew her work had been completed. It would be less painful to stay behind.

“Anything,” he replied.

“I’m redecorating your apartment.” In that much, she was certain.

Chapter 21

Pliny and Aelia sat on a couch in an isolated corner of the observation deck, hand in hand. It was just after the evening meal and the area was filled with couples hoping to see their first glimpse of the singularity. Pliny squeezed her hand, and she returned the action. His insides felt like they'd been blown up and reconstructed—the pain for almost losing Aelia to a difference in dogma still lingered. He had come so close to being accepted for who he was, only to self-destruct in the face of an apparent blasphemy.

"This is nice," he said.

"Indeed," she replied, rubbing her eyes.

"Do you think it's visible yet?"

"There's nothing up ahead. Or is there?" she asked, raising an eyebrow.

"Hard to say, really. We should have stuck with my room and we'd know for sure," Pliny said, peering off into the distance. It does seem as though there are stars missing, dead ahead."

"You're crazy," she said.

"In that, I have no doubt," he agreed with a smile. "I never finished telling you about my experience, did I?"

"No, we always get interrupted," she replied.

Pliny stretched. "I mentioned that I saw something while I was in surgery, right?"

"Right."

"I saw a swirling black and red mass, with gusts of flame coming from its poles and surrounded by a spinning red disc. It was very distressing," he said.

"So distressing that you broke off your relationship with the arbiters of absolute truth?"

"I thought we weren't going to get back into this," Pliny said, sighing.

"It needs to be said."

"I had no answers. I even saw a priest of Pluto to explain what I saw, and there were no answers. I needed to cast a wide net. I needed to find my soul."

"We all have a soul, Pliny," Aelia said, pulling her hand back.

"What happens after we die? I saw something, unlike anything I'd ever seen before. I wanted to be whole again. I felt like I was in another person's body. Expecting things to taste and feel the same, but the experiences were hollow. What was I to do?" Inside, he knew no God was the arbiter of reconstructive surgery. That was a human concern.

"Trust in the doctors, and the experts who say there are no ethical concerns to the procedure, then see to your devotions and meditate. You will find all you need there," Aelia said. She turned to fix her gaze on him, her gray eyes appearing to stare into his fractured soul.

"It's more difficult than it sounds," Pliny said.

"Did you talk to any friends about it?" she asked.

"Yes, I even made a few friends along the way."

"Interesting, you're bringing people together to investigate this?"

"Yes and no, I just wanted alternate viewpoints. Like the priest I went to thought I'd seen the gates of the realm of the dead. My sister thinks I'm crazy. A philosopher friend goes on about the inter-connectives of humanity, and a colleague wants to know what being dead feels like." He shrugged. "It's all relative, all I know is that I'm here, and this trip is helping me move on with my life." Pliny stretched, reaching over her shoulder and pulling her tight against him. She was so tiny compared to him, delicate and petite. The hair on the back of her neck tickled the crook of his elbow. He breathed deep, savoring the bouquet of her perfume. "You know what?"

"What?" She fidgeted, turning her eagle's gaze away.

"I'll write that book. Maybe nobody will ever read it, but the exercise may help me set the record straight."

"Is there anything I can do to help?" she asked.

"I suppose I could bounce ideas off you. But I don't even know where to start."

"From the beginning, I would think."

He sighed and squeezed her shoulder. "All right, now you have a job once we get back home. Hope you enjoy writerly angst."

"I've created a thing or two in my time; don't worry about it. This is about you, Pliny."

"You're right. This is all about me. My life, my struggle, my world." He smiled.

"So you'll do it? I need to see this through you, see how you came to your conclusions. I can help you, draw out the questions that need answering. Human resources taught me to see into a person's character, and judge the quality of an individual's truth," she said.

"I guess that's right on the mark for a human resources interviewer."

"And I'm damn good at what I do. Don't forget that for a second."

Pliny leaned back against the couch, enjoying its softness. He smiled, his eyes moving from Aelia to the void of space. The stars moved, but the center of their field of view was the purest black he'd ever seen, lined by a ring of warped stars. This was a space that no light escaped from. It was the singularity.

Chapter 22

Pliny sat on the small sofa in his room, holo-display turned on. What he saw was a light show that put Saturnalia's fireworks to shame. Every color imaginable emanated from the screen, tabs of mental notes, experiences, and philosophical ramblings danced together. He just needed to bring sense to it all. He'd switched his room's windows to show the x-ray spectrum, giving a fabulous vista. The black hole was a looming red object, with eruptions at both poles. The whole thing swirled, like flames in a bonfire. Pliny focused on it, taking a momentary pause from his work. The brain backup was proceeding as he worked. He didn't want to lose his momentum if something were to happen to him. *Would that only leave me with a quarter of a soul?* he asked himself, trying to suppress a shudder.

He let his thoughts turn to Aelia. He couldn't understand her extreme reaction to his problem—his issues hadn't called anyone's faith into question. Why did it bother her so much? He supposed it could be a fear of the Imperial Pantheon and their overzealous nature. Many did fear them, and spoke only in hushed tones about forbidden subjects and littered their homes with idols, as he once did. Such was life under a theocracy.

His book was coming along quite nicely. He knew the facts,

the hard points and exactly where to self-censor. It was a simple equation, easy for someone with a logical mind. He doubted anyone would be interested, but it was an exercise in concentration and creativity for him. He could always forward a copy to Tetra. She might appreciate it, even if Aelia did not.

The doorbell buzzed, yanking him out of his daydream of being a creative philosopher and back to reality. He shut down the projector and asked the computer to open the door as the room plunged into darkness.

Aelia stepped in. "Hi, Pliny," she began, before taking a look at the view outside his window. "That's sure viewing it a different way, right?"

"Yes, I'm looking at the x-rays it's putting out. Isn't it beautiful?"

"It certainly is evocative. Is that what you saw?" she asked, stepping further into the room.

"Very close to it," he replied.

"But what does that mean? People don't just *see* black holes. It doesn't happen, not even on a cruise like this one."

"I'm keeping an open mind here. It's not like the computer at the hospital knows anything about the human cost of reconstructive brain surgery."

"True, but you'd think they'd be prepared with answers to questions that might arise afterward."

Pliny shrugged. "Come in, sit down and enjoy the view. We can talk about the meaning of my life later. I just want to enjoy a moment with you. No ulterior motives, no affronts to our Gods."

She drew in, gracefully settling down onto the unyielding seat of the sofa. Her simple-yet-elegant red dress exposed her narrow shoulders, and her hair flowed around her face, framing her petite features.

He wrapped his arm around her shoulder and brushed the hair back from her face with his free hand. "You're so beautiful," he said, gazing into her deep brown eyes.

She lowered her head. "Thank you," she said.

He ran his hand through her hair, its silken strands sliding through his fingers. Even a small touch, like this, was ecstasy. He needed more, wanted more. Pliny moved his hand under her chin, moving her face to his. She looked up at him, her lips parting. They came together, like one being with one purpose—the moment lasted an instant, but their relationship suddenly changed.

Aelia pulled back, her hot breath tickling his face. "Wow, that was unexpected," she said.

"But it was so right. Everything is right with you, Aelia."

"I just need a little space. This is intense. I've never met another person like you, Pliny."

Pliny leaned back, his eyebrows shooting up. "It was just a kiss!"

"I know, I was just not expecting it."

"And now you're okay with it?"

"It was great and wonderful, but let's keep it going slow. I'm already out of my element being off-world. I don't want to make things awkward for the next ten days," she said.

"We have plenty of time to get it right, if that's how you feel."

"Yes, let's do it slow. How about an early dinner at the pub?"

"Okay. And after maybe spend some time in the observation lounge for some Zimmer 4007 and conversation?"

"Nothing would make me happier," Aelia said.

Chapter 23

Aelia sat in her quarters, nursing an unhappy stomach. She'd excused herself once the bottle of wine had been depleted, and told Pliny she was tired. She didn't know what to do. She could barely remember who she was—her core persona was melting around the feelings that twisted in her belly. He'd kissed her, and worse still, she enjoyed it!

She turned the lights on with a flick of her wrist, a trick she'd learned early on. She didn't trust her voice. Her body was shaking and she felt a touch dizzy. She cupped her hands over her mouth and took slow, deliberate breaths. She'd succeeded in her mission, but she didn't like this outcome. She wished she could take back her suggestion of writing a book. Pliny would implicate himself by his own hand. She would get lauded for her achievement and be pushed along for an eventual promotion. But, was that what she wanted now?

She rubbed her eyes. Why did he have to be cute, charming, and funny? He was interesting to talk to, even though his chosen occupation terrified her. She hoped that the concept of gray goo would fade from her consciousness. If he wasn't fast enough, could picobots assimilate all of Roma IV? The question disturbed her even more than her professional dilemma.

She needed guidance, a confidant who would keep her on the right path. She needed certainty, and she knew just how to get it.

Aelia willed her holo-screen to life, initiating a brain backup to accompany the transmission. She called home, to the Pantheon. To her Mistress. She hoped the powerful woman was in a good mood, because Aelia was in desperate need of guidance.

Marcia's face flickered to life, a wry smile gracing her ageless face. "Ah, Aelia, I was just wondering about your progress. It's good that you contacted me first."

"Mistress," Aelia said, bowing her head.

"Tell me everything."

"I have succeeded in my task," Aelia said.

"So shall I have a task force take him in at the spacedock?"

"There's more, though."

Marcia raised an eyebrow. "Oh?"

"He's writing a book outlining his thoughts and theories about the meaning of his experiences, and tying them into a larger world philosophy." Aelia spat the words out, her hands trembling in her lap.

"Interesting. I sense your delicate hand in this, am I correct."

Aelia nodded. "It was my idea, yes."

"Have you grown close?"

Aelia rubbed her eye. "Too close, Mistress."

"Remember your mission. All will be well once you're home again. Don't let one heretic spoil a challenging and rewarding career."

"How do you do it, Mistress Marcia?"

"When I was an Inquisitor, I'd been sent to ferret out a man not dissimilar to your Pliny. He was funny, personable, handsome, all of the noteworthy distractions of our species. Turning him in was the hardest thing I'd ever had to do, but we need to be strong as a culture. Only together in our belief and with an iron hand can we bring about our ultimate destiny as a galactic power, sweeping all others before us," the Mistress said, sweeping an arm over her imposing ebony desk.

"I understand."

"That gratifies me. You say it with such conviction and grace. All will be well, Aelia. I'll ensure that your needs are met post-mission."

Aelia smiled. Her heart raced. A promotion? More influence? The ability to make policy, rather than being the instrument that doles out punishments? "You are most generous, my Mistress. There is one further thing. He may have accomplices and associates, individuals who are inspiring and encouraging him. We may need to broaden our search."

"Fastidious to a fault, Aelia. We shall hunt them down and make an example of them. These people of the singularity will learn their role in a civilized society."

"People of the singularity are one thing. I recommend further restricting some elements of philosophical reasoning, as his work heavily borrows from articles downloaded through an academic network," Aelia added.

"Academics, burn them all. To Pluto with them! I am sick to death of those navel-gazers. All they do is push the limits of our security as a planet and offer nothing in return." Marcia rubbed her forehead. "I wish our Emperor would give us the power to close off non-scientific investigations into the nature of the universe. Jupiter gives us the will and strength to overcome all."

"Yes, Mistress."

"You're not … developing feelings for him, are you?"

"Our relationship is complex. I believe he is interested in me, and the lines between professional and personal are becoming fuzzy," Aelia admitted.

"It is good that you contacted me before you lost yourself in this situation. I gave you this mission because you're my best junior operative. Do not get attached—it will dampen your triumphant return to the order. Do you understand?"

"Completely, Mistress."

"Contact me if there is anything else you need. I shall send someone to pick you up at the spaceport to avoid any awkwardness on your behalf. Now, relax and enjoy the view. Of nothing. I don't understand why these cruises are so popular."

Aelia smiled, and the screen winked out. She could survive. Another seven days and she would be free of this situation and back home with her duties and her friends.

Chapter 24

A deep voice filled Pliny's chambers, drawing him out of his reverie and back into the real world. "All passengers: we have achieved a stable orbit around black hole Tau-Omega. It will be viewable through the entirety of the ship's observation lounges and cabins. Ask a server about all viewing possibilities, and enjoy yourselves."

Pliny shrugged and continued working, the red inferno of the black hole burning across the entirety of his window. He'd seen the black hole for days now. Going to the observation deck to look at the absence of life seemed like a waste. He needed this view, this perspective. It was the only thing that made sense to him now. As far as his work was progressing, it was as though a muse had perched on his shoulder. When Aelia rebuffed his advances, his future had once again become cloudy. What was her problem? What was his? He didn't know anymore. It wasn't like him to strike out—his track record was extremely positive when romantic partners were concerned.

He sighed and turned back to his work. He needed those files from Tetra. He needed that glue to tie the tapestry of his work together. He had an idea: he could contact her and have her send him what he needed. That material would be a welcome diversion from pining over Aelia. Tetra was attractive and intelligent, and she possessed an open mind. Despite Aelia's other obvious qualities, she was no intellectual.

He closed his documents and willed up his communications relay. The room's hidden holo-screen erupted in color, a blank screen materialized in the center of his room. He instructed the computer to give him Tetra's contacts, and then he initiated the call.

Tetra's face lit up the screen, a surprised smile on her face. Her brow drew upwards. "Pliny? What a treat," she said. "I thought you'd forgotten our very interesting night together."

"Now, Tetra, how could I? Sorry I haven't called, I've been on vacation."

"That explains the change in decor," she replied. "You like black now?"

"Always, but I called to tell you I've decided to write a book about my experiences," Pliny said.

Tetra clasped her hands over her mouth. "No way! Can I read it?" she asked.

"I have to finish it first. I have the general concept I want, but I need ideas. Philosophies. The concepts that glue life together and give it meaning."

"I happen to know a gatekeeper to such wisdom," she winked.

"Do you, now?" Pliny grinned, in spite of himself. Thoughts of Aelia faded, though his heart still ached.

"Yes, but first, tell me about your vacation. You never mentioned it to me," she said.

Pliny chuckled. "I'm on a black hole cruise. I was able to get a discount through a friend."

"You should have told me. I'd love to take that cruise." She held her hand over her mouth.

"I hadn't thought that much about it, this was a last-minute thing," Pliny said.

"Fair enough. What do you want from me?" she asked.

"Just the texts that we discussed. Maybe a friendly ear once I get home. It's all coming together and I need someone with an open mind to bounce my ideas off." Pliny glanced over his shoulder at the door, but there was only silence from the hall.

"Bounce away. When will you be back in town?"

"About a week. We're going to orbit the singularity for a few days and then we're coming back."

"And you're sitting in your room alone, when there's something invisible and deadly to view?" she said, playing with her red and black streaked hair.

"I get the same view from my quarters, without the exposure to small children and competition for the better sofas," Pliny said. "They even have alternate viewing modes, for the curious among us."

"Wish I was there, but this stupid paper of mine won't write itself. Send me a list of what you need and I'll clandestinely forward it to you." She arched an eyebrow. "I have my secrets."

"Will do, and there's always the possibility of a next time, right?"

"I have no doubt of that," she replied before closing the link.

Pliny smiled. No doubt at all. Felix once said something about closing and opening doors after being broken up with, and Pliny finally understood what his friend had meant.

Chapter 25

Pliny was putting the finishing touches to his latest chapter when the doorbell buzzed. He'd been shut in his little cabin for what seemed like weeks, working and observing. He hadn't seen anything of Aelia for days, and he distracted himself from that problem by throwing himself into his work. Work could be salvaged—made into something useful that served a purpose. It had been just one kiss. What was the damn issue with a kiss? They were both adults, everything should be easy, with the hysterics left for school-aged children. He sighed and allowed the door to open, turning his head to see who was there.

It was Aelia who stood just inside the entrance, wearing the same stunning red dress as when they first met. A braid hung over her left shoulder and her hands were clasped behind her back. "Can I come in?" she asked.

Pliny waved her in, catching her taking a long glance at his workscreen. He willed it out of sight. "What can I do for you?" he asked.

"I want to make things right," she said. "I know I judged you unfairly, but I want to move on and I'd like to continue where we left off. I was scared. I'm not the best with romance."

"So it seems."

"We fit so well together. Join me at the pub tonight, just like last week. The cruise isn't worth it if you're alone all the time and not making memories."

"I see your point. I suppose my book can wait, I'll take a break for a few hours," he said. Pliny stood, rolling his shoulders. The lights in the room went out as he sauntered to the door. He offered his arm to Aelia, which she took. "The *Void Star's* pub isn't quite as good as Aurora's back home, but it will have to do."

***

Pliny savored his platter of classic old Earth style deep-fried food, an assortment of hot peppers stuffed with cheese, cheese-stuffed breaded sticks, and a side of uncooked cheese. He was in a strange mood, perhaps not unlike a nervous teenager on his first date. He played with his food, moving it around the plate, trying to shape the pieces into some semblance of order.

Aelia spoke up. "You've barely said a word and you're playing with your food. What's on your mind?"

"Just the darkness in between us, as a species. We're so ugly to each other, when we're really all so similar. It doesn't make sense to me anymore. There has to be something that binds us together. A real experience, or a decisive fact of our universe."

"We all suffer and die," Aelia said plainly.

"Yes, and that's just the problem. Are we all headed to Pluto's realm, or is there something even more fundamental than that? The philosophies don't line up."

"That's a question as old as time. Why do you think you're going to advance humanity's understanding of the laws of nature and the interconnectedness of humanity?"

"No, just my own," he said.

"Then what's the point?"

"I *need* to know. It's all I see when I close my eyes. It's all I can taste when I eat. My feelings are empty. I need to reclaim my spirit and return myself to someone normal and functional again. I can't just go back to the goo factory and wait on picobots all day after the experience I had."

"What about your friends?"

"What about them? They're just curious, no harm in that right?" Pliny asked.

"Depends where it takes you, I suppose,"Aelia said.

"I don't expect anyone will be killing themselves for an opportunity to see what I saw. That's preposterous," Pliny said.

"But would you?"

"Truth be told, I had thought about it."

Aelia's jaw dropped. "Why would you even contemplate such a thing, just to revisit that?"

"I felt lost. Nobody would listen to me and I... I didn't feel right."

"You're okay now, though?" she said, reaching over the table to take his hand.

Pliny squeezed her fingers and took her hand between his. "Yes."

"I have something to confess," Aelia said.

Pliny froze. What could she have to hide? "Go on," he said.

"I'd never kissed anyone before that night," she said, her head hanging.

It all made sense to him now—the awkwardness, the slow pace, the unnatural progression of their relationship. "I see," he replied.

"I just got so tied up in my studies and my career that I didn't make time for the romantic stuff. All I wanted to do was go home and sleep."

"But, I can't believe you were never approached. You're one

of the most stunning women I have ever met," he said, picking up the bottle of wine and offering her a refill.

A redness erupted on Aelia's cheeks and her palm became damp. She nodded towards her empty glass. "There were people interested, but I never could tell if they were just being nice or not, or if I even liked them. My friends always called me the ice queen."

"You're nothing of the sort. We can take everything at the pace you need. No pressure, no tricks. Let's just enjoy each other's company for the remainder of the trip."

She raised her refilled glass. "To what is to come," she said.

Chapter 26

Pliny relaxed on his sofa and watched the stars fly across his line of sight. The cruise began its homeward journey two days before, and he was bored. His book was largely outlined, needing only input from Tetra over the nature of logic and the issue of a human singularity. The *Void Star* was heading toward home—the place where he'd been born, raised, and most recently died. *And a fortunate reincarnation*, he thought.

He was mulling over inviting people to his home once he arrived. He had much to share, to discuss. His cruise experience had been like going to the library and finding the best book to have ever completely surmised the human experience, only he'd lived it. This cruise had cemented his belief that humans are not simply lonely existential beings, doomed to lives of terrible solitude. Humans were more alike than dissimilar, in ways other than DNA. *We could all get along and understand each other, if we knew how.* His book could show just that, and he hoped its message would bring people together and make life on Roma IV a better and much kinder place.

Pliny didn't know what to make of going home. The cruise had been enjoyable, but the travel time had him at a loose end, and no relaxation could be had with screaming children in the observation lounge. He got an identical view here, in his quarters. Who cared if he saw Roma IV's planet-spanning archipelago first? He'd seen movies and simulations of it ever since he was a child. It wasn't something that would shatter his preconceptions of the universe, unlike the black hole.

Pliny got up and paced the room. He thought of Aelia—what was she doing? Was she lonely or bored? What was she going home to? Was there room for him in her busy life? Would she even want to try for a future with him? A future without Aelia seemed bleak and lonely, even with the interest of someone like Tetra. He sighed.

He moved to the door, stretching his back and chest on the way. A walk would do him good. He needed to stretch his legs after spending days in his closet of a room. He made his way to the observation deck, if only to remind himself of why he'd been hiding in his room for days. Was he really hiding from unruly children hyped up on sugar and boredom, or was he hiding from Aelia? *Only one way to find out*, he thought.

The air outside his room was noticeably fresher and cooler than that in his cabin, and he drew in one deep breath after another. He couldn't wait to walk by the sea and enjoy the briny winds and warm sun once again. The *Void Star* had its pleasures and some good restaurants, but home and Aurora's was where he wanted to be. He wanted to share wine with Tetra, banter with Felix and tell Gaius about the cruise, and thank him personally for his part in giving Pliny the opportunity of a lifetime.

The hallways were dim—little lights along the ceiling were the only hint that life existed at all on the ship. He navigated the darkness, holding out the hope for a view of home. He even missed his goo work for reasons that were beyond him. He suspected that it was the decent paycheck and automatic nature of the job he was missing. It was like babysitting, but with picobots. At least the bots were quiet and predictable. Unlike people, with all their spontaneity.

He stepped through an automatic door and the grandiose observation deck expanded into his field of view. The rows of couches, the strategically placed bars and the soothing classical music backdrop brought him back into the moment. He smiled, looking out the window. There was a star dead ahead—one bigger than all the others. Could that be home? That precious place where he planned to live out the rest of his life with a modicum of clarity. He hadn't even spoken to his sister recently. He would have to remedy that, and gauge her reaction to the life-sized statue of Venus he'd bought her for her birthday. *That will keep her in check*, he thought.

The stars continued their march across his peripheral vision. Tomorrow, they would make planet fall. He'd pick up his car and go back to his life. Entertaining ladies in his kitchen, studying in the library, and perhaps even taking a course at the university. Life was so rich, even missing a part of his soul. He'd come to realize that it wasn't in the nature of a soul to be divisible. You either had one or you didn't. Death was nothing more than a temporary inconvenience these past few centuries, if one could afford the treatments.

Leaning heavily against the railing, he moved to push his hand against the glass window. A force field crackled to life, pressing against his hand. Try as he might, he could not budge or move closer to the surface. He couldn't even leave a hand print on the windows, so insular was his existence on the *Void Star*. It really was like leaving nothing behind, only keeping the memories that he'd shared with many others. All would be preserved with him, in memory. He looked forward to savoring the events of the cruise from the comfort of home, courtesy of his memory backup. He considered adding impermanence to his book—he'd read about it in one of Tetra's historical papers, and it seemed like a good way to express the human condition.

A tap on his shoulder shook him from his reverie "Pliny, why are you trying to touch the glass?" Aelia said.

"I just wanted to see if I could," he replied. "I wanted to know if I'd leave a mark."

"You leave behind more than you think," she replied.

Pliny turned around, leaning his back against the bar. "What brings you out here?"

"Just catching some exercise. The common rooms are either awfully dull, or far too noisy."

"My thoughts exactly. I just wanted to breathe some different canned air."

"I feel the same way. Want to hit the pub for a last hurrah?" Aelia asked.

Pliny offered his hand. "Why should it be the last?" he asked.

Aelia smiled. "It doesn't have to be the last."

Pliny considered inviting her to his apartment after they landed. He was already planning a small gathering of his philosophical friends. Perhaps she'd be more at ease with his thinking if she realized he wasn't alone with his thoughts. "Say, do you have any plans after planet fall?"

"Just going home and breathing real air and seeing daylight."

"Why not come to my place? I'll be having a small party with my friends in a couple of days. You can meet everyone and you can help me redecorate."

She grinned. "All right, you've convinced me. Give me a date and time and I'll come crash your party with my excellent eye for good taste and an uncanny feel for idolatry."

"You're on. Just don't get jealous of my statue of Minerva."

Chapter 27

The sun hit Pliny square in the eyes the moment he stepped off the *Void Star*. He reflexively blinked, raising a hand to shield his light-sensitive eyes. Another unexpected thing about this trip, he mused. The brine of the sea flooded into his nostrils, and he sucked in a deep breath, followed by three others in quick succession. He smiled, enjoying the heat on his skin and the fresh air in his lungs. He moved across the causeway into the spaceport, not turning back to give the *Void Star* one last look. He'd taken the trip, seen the black hole and even written some of a book in the process. In a few nights, he'd hold a small party at his home, describing his experience to his friends. Perhaps even Claudia would attend, if she was in a supportive mood.

Aelia was nowhere to be found, but he considered the possibility that they could have been let out in groups. He had her contact, and he expected that she would join his party, meeting his friends and telling them about her experience on the cruise. He especially wanted to show her off to his highly religious sister, as proof that he had what it took to get a moral woman. He ran a hand through his hair, and looked around. His baggage was circulating on a conveyor belt. As he walked towards the luggage, he remarked that the open-air spaceport let the natural light illuminate it like a great cathedral of the stars. Perhaps he would return, someday.

If the sun was to be revered, as they did with the binary stars on Horus III, why then would it not be possible to revere a black hole? It was, after all, a singularity. A unique point in space that pulled in all that was unfortunate enough to wander into his path. That was true power.

He grabbed his wheeled bag, and pulled it towards where he'd parked his car. The walkway was automatic, and he let the machine do the work for him as he searched the crowd for Aelia. His heart sank as he realized that she had probably left before him, as her room was on a much lower deck. He stepped off the conveyor belt and headed for the car lot. His car was there, undamaged and untouched. He slid onto the driver's seat and willed it to life, the holographic controls dancing in front of him. He directed the machine to take him home, and left it on auto-pilot while he let his mind wander.

The city zoomed past as he gazed out the window. Back to work tomorrow, which would give him the grounding he needed to muddle through his life and projects. Of course, the money would be nice. He needed to focus more on his health and being able to afford the proverbial fountain of youth that was available through modern medicine. But, that was a concern for another time. Low houses rushed past, all in white brick or stone. Black shingled roofs topped each one. The uniformity bored him, and he wished he could afford one of the unique buildings in the old city. But, it was a choice. He could have youth and brain backups, or that beautiful old red brick house he'd been eyeing for the past decade. There were just too many things to do and desire in life, and choices had to be made.

He closed his eyes, remembering his and Aelia's time together. He was disappointed that he didn't get to properly say goodbye. All he had was her name and her contact. He just had to trust that the universe would unfold as he hoped it would but with a woman as passionate and beautiful as her, competition would be fierce. All he had to offer was a half-baked philosophy and a boring job.

The car obediently pulled into his parking stop, the buzz of the hovercraft humming as he bobbed over the pavement. He stepped out, into the heat of the sun. His building lay dead ahead and his apartment on the top floor beckoned. A lonely, empty apartment with no idols and nothing but a noose to meditate on. He took his bags from the back seat, and with a thought the car settled onto its landing frame. The area was quiet, not a soul could be seen or heard.

Pliny trudged up the stairs, the lightly floral scent in the halls replacing the soothing balm of the sea. Finally, his door loomed before him, and he picked up the pace. He needed his brain backup unit, his notes, and a quiet evening in, watching *Minerva Colosseum*. He walked into the bedroom and deposited his items on the bed. He'd deal with that later. He went into his empty living room and sat on the recliner. There was no equivalent to the simple comforts of home.

Pliny willed his holo-display to activate, the lights reflected off his bare walls and information flooded into his senses. He commanded it to open a channel to his sister. Her face appeared on the screen, mouth twisted down into the picture of annoyance. "Brother, how good of you to finally return my calls," she said.

"I took a trip," he began before getting cut off.

"So you mean to say that you didn't see fit to tell your next of kin that you were going off on a vacation? How typical of you."

"It's not like that! It was a really last minute thing. And it was the opportunity of a lifetime."

She palmed her face. "What was it?"

"A black hole cruise."

"Goodbye."

Pliny reached towards the screen. "Wait, there's more! I met someone."

"You, and a someone? This has to be rich."

"She's passionate, she's bright, driven, and, as you would say, *moral*."

"All that and she picked you?" Claudia asked.

"Will wonders never cease?"

"In that case, I forgive you, this time. Don't go blowing your chances with her with all your seditious lies against the Pantheon." Claudia's blond curls bounced as she shook her head.

"That's all in the past now. She said she'd help me properly redecorate my home."

"So you've come back to the side of reason."

"I wasn't aware that I had ever left."

"Sometimes you worry me, big brother."

Claudia closed the connection, leaving Pliny with his thoughts. Could his sister be reasoned with at all? He didn't like the possibility that her hostility would eventually drive the old wedge back between them. He loved his sister, despite her faults and failings. He'd fought hard to maintain a relationship with her —a one-sided endeavor that was never reciprocated. He sighed.

There was a party to plan, and he set about ordering the food and wine to make it happen.

Chapter 28

Aelia sat silently in the car as her escort guided it along the road to the headquarters of the Imperial Pantheon. The towering monstrosity that was the Temple of Pluto loomed in the distance, its impossible obsidian black tower scraping the clouds. Office buildings flanked both sides of the busy boulevard. Thoughts and regrets fought a battle in her mind. She clutched her arms across her chest and her palms were sweaty. She didn't want to face her Mistress, didn't want to perform her ultimate duty, which would destroy Pliny.

She needed to be the one to bring Pliny and his associates in. Then she would have closure and the admiration of the Pantheon. Work should be a reward in and of itself, right?

Every heaving breath brought her closer to the palace, with its immense nude pillars of Atlas supporting the vast ceiling. She didn't want to have to look at the statues. They would remind her of Pliny and her own failure as a woman. She hadn't realized how difficult meeting a good person would be, until he'd been dropped in her lap. Why did they have to be so diametrically opposed with regard to moral standards? He'd caused her to question her worldview—a feat that had never been accomplished before, even after torturing heretics for confessions. *Unless they were simply afraid of me*, she thought.

The car slowed, then hovered at the gates of the temple. The place was unchanged, but its mammoth proportions overwhelmed her even more than the size of the grandiose *Void Star*. She strode to the wooden entry doors and pushed them open. The smell of fragrant incense and wood flooded her nose, taking her back to her days as an acolyte tending to the incense burners and cleaning the statues in her off-hours when she wasn't in training. Now she was questioning her life goals. To abandon a thriving career for a man was unheard of. Nobody, to her knowledge had ever left the service of the Pantheon.

The accusing face of Atlas stared down from the pillars as she made her way through the grand chamber. The constellations haunted her peripheral vision and Atlas seemed in judgment of her for her actions on the cruise. Could the Gods really come back if their servants were so fragile?

She swallowed as she approached the ebony door that lay between her and Mistress Marcia. She placed her hand on the knocker, the sound echoing through the palatial chamber.

"Come in," a voice blared through a speaker next to the door.

Aelia pushed the door and stepped inside, allowing herself time to close the door behind her. No prying eyes would witness her failure. She dropped to her knees, her head bowed. "Mistress."

"Rise, young one, and come closer," the Mistress said.

Aelia got to her feet and strode to the giant ebony desk. "It is good to see you again, my lady."

"This was not an easy assignment. Are you ready for your next one?"

Aelia straightened. "Anything. I am ready."

"Do you have the strength to follow through on the consequences of your last mission?" Marcia's eyes bored into Aelia, as though seeing her very soul.

Aelia swallowed. "I can do it."

"Then you shall be elevated to the rank of Junior Executor, and you shall root out this rat's nest yourself. Bring me Pliny and his co-conspirators. I realize this is a difficult task for someone just coming into their twenties, but I need to see your dedication."

"Yes, Mistress."

"No lingering emotions are permitted. This is for the benefit of our society as a whole. One man can poison an entire district."

"I know, Mistress. I shall attend their clandestine gathering and compel them to come with me."

Marcia stood, her flowing purple dress moving with the form of her body. She reached below her desk, and pulled out an ornate staff made of ebony. "Enjoy the fruits of your labor, Executor. Make us proud."

Aelia took the rod, and her heart sank. It was real. This promotion had been what she always wanted, but now she very much wanted to be someone else. "Thank you," she said.

"Do not disappoint me. Now go," Marcia said as she settled back into her chair.

Aelia took her staff and left. She needed to get new clothes and fresh makeup to fit her new rank, to play the part she'd have for the rest of her life.

Chapter 29

Pliny stood behind his marble counter top, basting a giant Roma dodo and breathing in the rich scent of the large bird. His mouth watered in anticipation as he eased it back into the oven. Felix lounged on the couch while Gaius remained standing. Tetra hadn't yet arrived, and she was supposed to bring the wine. There was always wine at these sorts of gatherings, and there was never enough when it came to reveling with friends. Felix and Gaius were happily discussing the implications of consciousness with regard to death, and this pleased Pliny. He always liked bringing people together, especially from different facets of his life.

The doorbell rang. He looked to the camera—it was Tetra. He smiled and she waved a bottle of wine up in front of the camera. Without a second thought, Pliny admitted her. His heart raced. What would Tetra and Aelia think of each other? Would they get along or compete for his attention? He fervently hoped that the cosmos would align itself into an order favorable to his self-interest.

There was a knock at the door, and he willed the portal open. In stepped Tetra wearing a striped purple dress with a flashy silver necklace that supported a bull's head. She carried a bag filled with wine bottles and promptly walked up to the table and offloaded her contribution onto the counter. "Gentleman, I have brought us all a treat. Zimmer 4007, fresh from the vineyard's reserves."

"Nice," Felix said, before turning back to his conversation with Gaius.

Pliny pulled down some wine glasses from a high shelf, smiling. He was in his element—cooking for friends while enjoying a nice glass of red wine. It was easy and natural. Pliny enjoyed small, intimate gatherings, but this one was testing the limit of his comfort zone. Four people were a handful to keep satisfied and entertained, especially while managing a complex dish like Roma dodo.

Tetra filled the glasses one by one. Pliny took one and drew a long sniff. It was remarkable. Zimmer always put out quality wines, but 4007 was the best year yet. He took a sip and held it on his tongue while Tetra handed out the other glasses.

"Pliny," Felix said, raising a glass. "To your death and rebirth."

"I'll drink to that," Pliny said, laughing.

"You have most excellent friends and wonderful hospitality. Cheers!" Gaius added, taking a sip.

Pliny smiled. "I'm honored to have you all here. It's wonderful to have such supportive, intelligent friends. I look forward to telling you all about my trip and the lessons I learned along the way."

Without any warning, Claudia erupted into the room. She must have used the keycard he'd given her to get past the security protocols. "Hello big brother, miss me?" she asked.

"Of course," Pliny said.

"I didn't know you had a sister," Gaius said. "Are you single?" he asked.

"Yes and no, I could use a third," Claudia said, laughing.

"I'm intrigued," Felix said, looking up from his conversation with Tetra.

Claudia walked up to Pliny and embraced him. "I'm so glad you're feeling right again," she said.

An awkward pause followed.

"A bullet to the head will ruin anyone's sense of well-being," Tetra added, breaking the silence.

"True enough. Where's my wine?" Claudia asked.

Gaius walked to the counter and poured her a glass. She took it, savoring its bouquet and smiling.

"Let's have some fun. Where are your decorations?" Claudia asked.

"Check the closets. I'm looking to redecorate"

***

There was a knock at the door. Pliny checked the screen. It looked like Aelia's smiling face, but it was cast in shadows. He admitted her, knowing that she was the last invited guest. Smiling, he watched the door and waited for the bell to sound. After a pregnant pause it finally buzzed.

Immediately after admitting her, Pliny knew something wasn't right. She was wearing a long purple-striped robe and holding a scepter in her right hand. Her makeup was done with harsh lines outlining her eyes and accentuating the arches of her cheeks. Pliny's heart sank. She was an Executor. He'd been fooled and betrayed.

"Aelia," he began, and was promptly cut off.

"I am Executor Aelia of the Imperial Pantheon," she said. "You are all going to come with me. We can do this the easy way, or we can wait for my Liquidators and Sisters to hunt you down. Which will it be?"

Pliny stood mute, his mind racing in every direction and no direction at once. "You? An Executor? Is this a joke, Aelia?"

"So this is the moral woman you found?" Claudia shrieked. "Look at what you've done!"

Aelia pointed at him with her staff, its darkness rivaling pure obsidian. "I command you to come with me. All of you."

"No," Claudia said. "No, I'll wait for the Liquidators. I am a true believer and I condemn the rest of these fools for their lack of faith."

Felix spoke up: "Is this possible, Pliny?"

"I'm just a student!" Tetra protested. "My work is sanctioned by the Imperial Pantheon and I hold all the proper permits."

"That is irrelevant. You have been named as an accomplice. However, I can be convinced to be merciful," Aelia said. "Unless you prefer being practice for the trainee Inquisitors."

Pliny's heart raced. Mercy from an Executor. "How so? Aelia, please…"

"I do not wish for you to be brought before my Mistress, nor do I desire to continue living the life of a merciless Executor. I have seen that life can be beautiful and that the universe is more vast and wondrous than Gods who do not smile upon us." Aelia sighed. "I have a plan, if you could find it in your hearts to trust me. This is difficult to ask. I can't stop the Pantheon, but I can save the lot of you."

Pliny put down his wine glass, his hands shaking. "I'm guessing that the Liquidators don't offer terms."

"Indeed," Aelia said. "They exist to gather evidence and re-consecrate the location. If you're here when they arrive I cannot help you."

Claudia stormed out the door, her cheeks flushed red and hands balled into fists. "I'm out. The rest of you can burn. Never contact me again, Pliny. You're dead to the Gods, and to me." The door slammed, leaving Pliny with no time to react or plead. His life was over. No more evenings at Aurora's, no more goo factory, no more Saturnalias or sparring with Claudia.

"Damn," Gaius said. "What do we do?" He rubbed his eyes and sniffed. "Everything, everyone… my life…," he muttered.

"We get into my van and head to the spaceport. From there I commandeer a ship and we head for the Terran Federation seeking refugee status on grounds of religious persecution." Aelia spoke slowly, as though she were struggling with herself to articulate her thoughts.

"I think we don't have a choice," Pliny said, turning off the oven, sighing. "I'm ready to go. Are the rest of you coming?"

"No choice, glad I don't have a family for once," Felix said. "I regret ever meeting you, Pliny."

Pliny hung his head.

"Might as well take this as an opportunity to travel," replied Gaius. "Make the best of…this," he said, making a sweeping motion.

"The Terran universities are better anyways." Tetra said, walking over to the door. "I'm in. Let's go before I start crying, too." Her eyes were watery.

Aelia straightened. "Excellent. I'm parked outside. We've just enough time to get to the spaceport before we're missed."

They filed out, with Pliny in the rear. He turned back to look at his apartment, his pride and joy, one last time. The lingering smell of roasting bird danced in the air and he sighed as he commanded the door to lock. The Liquidators would need to work for their prize. He hoped they'd contemplate their life goals after finding the noose in his closet.

A black van hovered out front, and its side doors slid open as they approached. They piled in, and were squished together. Pliny sat on the edge of his seat, squeezed up against the side of the vehicle. Tetra was sandwiched between Pliny and Gaius.

The doors closed, and a locking mechanism audibly clicked. Pliny's heart stopped. Had it all been an act? Was Aelia really helping them escape?

Aelia pressed some buttons on the invisible console, and set the van in motion. She opened a channel. "Tell Mistress Marcia that I have the heretics and am transporting them now."

Pliny hung his head in silence. He had been such a fool. Not only had his naivete destroyed his life, but those around him. All these people he barely knew, good people, put in this terrible position.

He could never forgive himself.

Chapter 30

Aelia swallowed hard as the obsidian tower on the Temple of Pluto panned into view. If she went through with this, she'd never be entombed with her people, her order, and her gods. But, if there were no gods to speak of, then she was just dead at the end of it. Could she justify taking more life for something she herself questioned? She knew the answer and it shook her to the core of her being. She couldn't, and now every human she'd ever put to the question haunted her. Their cries and pleading for their lives, their family's lives, all of the knowledge extracted by her torture and painful neural scans. She had no future on Roma IV. The best she could hope for was being taken in by a Terran Federation world and retrained. Perhaps eventually, she would really become an interviewer for human resources.

She'd taken the van to manual settings and she drove on the backstreets. In a roundabout way, she was heading for the space dock. Her plan was fuzzy beyond that. Commandeer a ship and make a run for it? Stow-away and commandeer a life pod? No ships went close to Terran space—it was forbidden.

"Does anyone here know how to fly a ship?" she asked.

The silence was impenetrable. Gaius cleared his throat. "I've taken lessons."

"That will have to do. I have a plan," she replied.

"Do you, now?" Pliny spat the words out. "Other than turning me away from my home and family and betraying me?"

"I betrayed everything I ever was and hoped to be here. I left my career, my life, and my security for you." The final word erupted through her lips, and she scowled. "Do you want to know how to get out of this, or would you rather I turn us around and go back to my easy life of torturing you for a confession?"

"When you put it that way, tell us your brilliant plan, *Executor*," he said, his tone hard.

"We take a ship and fly to the Terran Federation. From there we claim to be members of a persecuted religious minority and seek asylum. Any questions?" she asked.

"Just one: how will we escape the seekers they send after us?" Gaius asked.

"We're going to steal a cruiser. One with a negative-space drive. They can't shoot what they can't connect with." Aelia explained.

"And you just happen to have one?" Tetra spoke up, raising her chin from her chest.

"I am an Executor. I have the scepter, and the power to take one."

"Of course you do," Felix said. "No one dares to deny you anything."

"Look, you can hate me all you want. I deserve it. But, I'm trying to make the best of a dangerous situation," Aelia said, glancing back at her passengers. Four sets of sullen, red eyes gazed dejectedly back at her.

"So, say I can fly a ship with a negative-space drive," Gaius asked. "How do we know which one to take?"

"We're going to steal the *Void Star*."

"That one's huge," Pliny said. "Why that one?"

"I know my way around it, and it has a negative-space drive

that will be helpful in evading pursuit," Aelia replied.

Gaius cleared his voice. "I've never flown a negative-space drive ship before."

"You'll learn," Aelia said.

"Too convenient, how can we trust you?" Felix asked.

Aelia sighed. "In that you have no choice."

Pliny cleared his voice. "What about my sister?"

"Pray for her, if you still believe in anything," came Aelia's reply.

"Did you give them her name?" Pliny asked.

"No. But, they can check your building's door logs. I'm sorry."

"Damn you."

***

The *Void Star* towered over them, its unmarked hull glistening in the afternoon light. The sea made its presence known, and a light breeze tickled the exposed flesh on Aelia's arms. She swallowed. Was this the last time the sun would kiss her skin and the sea prickle her nose? She hoped not, but her gamble had a low chance of success at best.

She squared her shoulders and walked up to the flight crew—a group of four people in orange coveralls and hard hats. She held her scepter out, pointing it at the supervisor. "I am Executor Aelia Vellus of the Imperial Pantheon. I need to quarantine the *Void Star* pending an examination by my liquidators."

The man paled, and took a step back. "Mistress, I can assure you," he said, before being cut off.

"Is this how you speak to a representative of the Theocracy? I am not joking. There is a hive of malcontents intent on boarding that ship and I intend to purge them from our society." She tried her best not to shake, and spat out every word as though it tasted of soured wine.

"Yes, Mistress," he said, his shoulders sagging. He motioned them to the front entrance. Its yawning portal seemed to swallow all light cast into it.

"We will search the general quarters. I will keep you posted. Seal the doors behind us. I will signal the base once we have caught our quarry," she said, still waving the ominous wooden staff. She hoped they would not question why the rest of her team were not in uniform.

"This won't reflect on us, will it?" the man asked, shifting his weight from foot to foot.

"You are trying my patience. Allow us access and afford us the respect our position commands. That is your final warning."

The man bowed his head. "As you command, Mistress." He herded his crew out of earshot.

Aelia was the first to cross the threshold, exchanging the fresh seaside air for recirculated air conditioning. A chill overcame her as the heat of the sun was swallowed to a memory.

The door slid shut. The corridor was silent. "Let's do this," she said, turning and nodding to her unhappy set of unlikely companions.

Chapter 31

Pliny sat in a chair on the bridge, in front of a console that held a holographic display. The meaning on the symbols in front of him were gibberish, all related to position, speed, relativistic distortion, and supposedly life-support. He wasn't sure why he was needed on the bridge. Aelia wouldn't let him out of her sight —clearly she didn't trust him on his own while they were working to launch the vessel without clearance or detection from the authorities.

"I've got it!" Gaius announced. "Felix and I have figured out the command codes, and the relativistic time drive will keep us out of sync with the normal pursuit spacecraft. I can scramble the codes once we've used them and that will keep them from retaking control. I'll leave access to the viewscreen, so we can talk to the Federation. That is where we're going, right?"

"Right. So we can strap down and launch?" Aelia said.

"Fortunately, we came onboard just after the kitchens had been replenished. We won't starve, at least," Tetra said. "Maybe we can get Pliny to cook for us."

"I'd be happy to," Pliny said. "Anything for the people whose lives I've ruined."

"You have a lot to make up for," Felix said. "I can't believe I got myself into this. I just wanted to know what being dead feels like!"

"Well, maybe if you didn't press so hard, I wouldn't have thought about it and we'd all be safe now," Pliny shot back.

Felix took a step toward Pliny, hands balled into fists. Tetra came between them, her arms outstretched. "Enough of this! It's done and we need to move on before the real agents arrive."

"Fine," Felix grumbled, stalking back to his chair on the other side of the room. The lighting was lower there, and he sulked in the shadows.

"Are we ready to launch, children? Aelia asked.

"Ready as we'll ever be," Gaius replied.

"Begin the launch sequence. The Terran Federation awaits."

***

The viewscreen flashed to life, projecting a stern-faced woman with gray hair. Her features were as timeless as the gods', and her scowl was enough to make Pliny sit upright in his chair. His heart raced—was this the patron Mistress of the Imperial Pantheon? Was she the one who had sealed his fate without even speaking to him or allowing him to plead his case? What kind of universe allowed for that kind of barbarity? He was surprised by the thought that his own people—and the people of countless generations before him—were barbarians. But, what else could a theocracy be?

The image moved, shaking him from his reverie. "Executor Aelia Vellus, explain yourself."

Aelia walked from her chair to the middle of the room. "I can no longer support the Pantheon in good faith. These people are no threat to the Gods, yet we persecute them. I can no longer be the one to put the innocent to the question."

"You foolish child. I was ready to give you the reins to true power, yet you throw it all away for a heretic."

"I make my own decisions now. I am Aelia Vellus, and I shall not be brought to heel by the Theocracy."

"Then die screaming alongside your new lover." The woman spat out the final word and closed the connection.

Aelia sighed, her shoulders stooped. "After a lifetime of duty, I get not even an attempt at hearing me out," she said.

Pliny turned to her. "You're doing what you think is right. There's no shame in that."

"I know, but—" she began, before getting cut off by Gaius.

"There are two ships moving to intercept from the surface!"

"Damn it!" Aelia said. "What are our options?"

"We increase speed until we clear the solar system, then make the jump with the negative-space drive. They shouldn't be able to interact with us once we're clear. They'd be fools to even attempt interference at that point," Gaius replied. Sweat was beading on his brow.

"Do it. Try to shake them—can we use the asteroids to mask our trail?"

"That's tricky," Gaius said. "This is a cruise liner, not a yacht or a warship. I think I can manage to get us lost, but at a major detriment to our speed. I barely even know what the controls do. I flew a simple orbiter back home, mostly in simulations."

"Do what you can."

"Do I have to call you 'Mistress'?"

"No, Aelia will do quite nicely."

Pliny sat, processing and re-processing everything that was said. He was cold. The shock of everything made him feel like he'd taken a boot to the gut. All of this was happening because of him, because he couldn't leave well enough alone.

"I'd like to say something," Pliny said.

Four sets of eyes looked around at him.

"I want to apologize. All this is my responsibility. I didn't intend on doing anyone any harm. I was simply curious, much as you all were regarding my experience."

Felix laughed while Gaius wiped his brow with the back of his hand. "I'll never see my friends or family again, thanks to you. My pets will die and some liquidator will purge and sell my house. How's that for a destroyed life?" Gaius asked.

The mutterings floated through the room. Pet's names, family members, jobs, projects—all discarded because of him. Pliny held his head in his hands, tears swelling up in his eyes. He couldn't deal with it, couldn't shoulder their ire and pain. He scrambled to his feet and rushed from the room through the observation lounge exit.

The lounge was exactly as he remembered it—palatial with a domed screen. Stars marched past, but not at the pace they'd followed on the cruise. He supposed that they hadn't yet entered interstellar space.

He withdrew to his old favorite couch at the center of the window and sat down, his elbows on his knees.

All he could do was cry.

Chapter 32

After Pliny left the room, Aelia was alone with her guilt. All of these people, destroyed as collateral damage. A gnawing sensation in her stomach was accented by every word, every tear. But, she could not leave her post, not until this small tribe was safe from her former master's forces. She clenched the arms of her seat, tensing one hand and then the other. She ruminated over the events of the past two weeks. How could she have fallen quickly and so completely, from devoted Inquisitor to heretic? Had she even truly believed, or was she simply a lonely, innocent orphan lead down a predetermined path by her handlers?

She rubbed an eye, noticing that Gaius was staring at her. She cocked her head and looked his way.

"The interceptors are only two minutes out!" he exclaimed.

"Can you lose them?" she asked.

"This isn't a space movie—this thing maneuvers slower than my bathtub."

"What are our options?"

"We don't have many, Aelia," Gaius said. "I can rock the ship a bit, to weaken their harpoons and their weapons. Just pray to whatever gods you still actually believe in that they are ordered to take us alive, rather than destroying us outright."

Aelia sighed. "Indeed. Do whatever you think best."

The ship rocked, sending them all off balance. Then a soundless disturbance vibrated through Aelia's bones, and she lurched in her chair.

"What the hell was that?" Tetra asked.

"They've hooked us with a harpoon!" Gaius shouted, frantically hammering on his display unit. Text flew by faster than Aelia could read.

"How much further to the border?" Aelia asked.

"We're about three hours out," Gaius replied.

"Activate the negative-space drive," Aelia commanded.

"What? That could destroy us!"

"Do we have any other options?" she asked, tugging on her braid.

"We could wiggle a bit, but that will affect us more than them. The inertial harpoons are dragging us back."

"Do you prefer to be tortured or lost between dimensions? Activate the damned drive."

He froze, and then sighed. "Yes, *Mistress*. Hang onto your seats everyone, this is going to get rough."

Aelia braced herself, clinging to the seat. She gulped down deep breaths in a desperate attempt to steel herself to the terror that was to come. Dizziness overwhelmed her senses, and she started shaking.

The ship lurched, and the stars raced towards them. Matter seemed to almost phase through them. The echoes of tiny rocks pelting the hull made her flinch. "What's the problem?"

"We're clear of our pursuers, but we're taking damage from the asteroid field. We should be clear in a few minutes. However, they might be braver, or dumber than we think."

"How so?"

They're still gaining on us, even though their inertial harpoons are ineffectual against the hull. They could use conventional weapons on us, or worse, plasma-blast us out of existence."

"Use your own discretion, Gaius," Aelia said. "Trust your instincts. Now, I shall go check on our fearless leader. We need to concoct something to request asylum over, and we need it fast."

***

Aelia strode to the observation lounge, and leaned against the door frame. She took a few deep breaths to center herself. She needed the old Aelia, the one who cut through dissent with a knife. But, rather than cut it out, she needed to carve it into a weapon to save them all. She didn't know how rigorous the Terrans were about their religious freedoms, but these people were their only hope. She composed herself, pulling her braid over her left shoulder. She walked over to the couch where she and Pliny had shared their dreams and aspirations. It was where she'd lost her faith, and where she'd find it once more. This time, however, it would be in a man rather than gods.

He was there, sitting slouched over with his head in his hands. She stood before him, casting a shadow over the seemingly-infinite stars of the Milky Way. "We need to talk," she said.

"Just leave me alone. I should have killed myself when I had the chance," he said.

"That's not who you are, Pliny," she said, taking a seat. She pulled one of his hands into hers. "There is still hope."

"How do you figure?"

"A wise person once told me, 'where's there life, there's hope,'" she replied.

"That person probably didn't piss off the Imperial Pantheon." He sighed.

"We can debate that later. For now, we need a plan. We need

to figure out what we're telling the Terran Empire. We know they're freer than we are, but we need something to work with. A name, some sort of article of faith. A scripture, do you follow?"

"I think so, yeah."

"Just think of everything that holds the Pantheon together, and give us an equivalent. The Terrans have been rescuing refugees for centuries."

"What do you know about the Terrans? How will we even be able to communicate? Our languages have taken different evolutionary paths since the dissolution," Pliny asked.

Aelia frowned. "I don't know much of them, other than the Mistress fears them more than Pluto himself. They're free, and they can speak and question freely. As for communications, I'm sure they've developed technology to facilitate that. They are an ingenious people."

"All right," he said. "I know what I need to do."

Chapter 33

Pliny scratched his bald spot as he took his seat on the bridge. Aelia stood next to him, her hand on his shoulder. The communication relay buzzed. "It's Mistress Marcia," Gaius said. "There are more ships headed our way!"

"Answer her," Aelia said.

Marcia's scowl and backing bookshelf flickered to life, her hands folded over an impossibly black desk. She dominated the ship's forward viewscreen. "Aelia, stop this madness. You know you'll never reach the Terran Federation. You know they'd never accept an orphan born into the Imperial Pantheon. Give up now, and I'll show some mercy to your friends. Only you need to die screaming."

"I find this offer unappealing, Mistress," Aelia swallowed in spite of herself. Her heart hammered in her chest. She felt very much the small orphan she was, one rescued from the steps of the very thing she had now betrayed.

"Oh, does the knowledge that I will personally put you to the question and make an example of you put the fear of the gods back in you?"

"Not at all. I have found a new calling, and I am my own woman, not that helpless baby abandoned on the steps of the

Pantheon's Imperial Palace. I decide my fate, not you." Aelia stood straighter as she spoke.

Pliny wrung his hands, and swallowed.

"More ships are on their way, with weapons that can defeat your special drive. Pray that you die by their hand and not mine."

"I shall do nothing of the sort,"Aelia answered.

"And to this young man, the one who can afford a brain backup but not hair replacement, what do you call yourself?"

Pliny stood up from his chair and squared his shoulders. It was time to declare his true identity. "I am Gothi Pliny Augur and I lead the Children of the Singularity. I am at your service, witch who cannot afford hair dye."

Marcia leaned back in her chair. "A Gothi? What in Pluto's realm is a Gothi? You follow one who gives himself airs, Aelia?"

"No, he gives me clarity, a place in a universe of connected souls and shared experience. We shall escape your net and take refuge with the Terran Federation. Our leader, this … Gothi will lead the way. Just like he did when he was graced with the vision of our collectiveness," Aelia replied.

"This is madness! Think, child."

"No, you are the one who is mad. I am following my heart and my soul."

"You are blinded by lust, that much is clear. The first man who ever pays attention to you and you run away from your duty."

"Clearly, you know nothing about me, or my heart." Aelia said.

Pliny wanted to hold the poor girl who stood next to him. Rejected by her parents and going against the only love and authority she'd ever experienced. What a challenge it must have been to her to even consider his thinking. How could his loss compare to the loss she was enduring? Could his death even make up for the harm he'd caused? He spoke up: "This accomplishes nothing. I am the true authority here, and I will never yield to a power that strips its citizens of the right to think."

The elderly woman paled and sat back for an instant. "Rights? We are enlightened by the grace of Emperor Vespasian II, and the gods bring glory to his name. We must all stand together to bring their favor upon us, and we shall use their powers to defeat the heretic planet of Horus III, and eventually, the entire Terran Federation. So it is written. Do you understand me, boy?"

"Whatever you say, Mistress. But what you say is no more than words."

Mistress Marcia flushed dark red, and Aelia's grip on his arm tightened.

"I will have you dead, Gothi Pliny, and I will torture you personally. Then you will learn the meaning of respect."

"I'd *love* to stay and chat, but I have a book to write and no time to waste with you," Pliny said, before motioning to Gaius to close the channel. "That went relatively well," he said.

"If she brings us in personally, that's both a good and a bad thing," Tetra said, wringing her hands.

"How do you figure?" Aelia asked.

"Its a lot more complicated for her to get us back to her alive. They'd have to stop the *Void Star*, board it, shut down the engines and arrest us personally. Dead is simply blowing us out of the sky, and by the sounds of things she's moved beyond that."

"Logical, as always," Pliny said.

"I try," Tetra replied, before turning back to the console in front of her. She pulled up the flight instructions for the *Void Star* and began reading.

"Let's put this unpleasantness behind us and concentrate on getting to the Terran Federation safely. How soon can we send them a signal that we're seeking asylum?" Pliny asked.

"About an hour for live-contact. This ship doesn't have up to the minute communications arrays. It's never been very far from home, I guess," Gaius said.

"Someone cut costs. But, we have to make the best out of this bathtub. Can we go any faster or deeper into negative-space with the time-drive?" Aelia asked.

Gaius paused for a moment, before Felix butted in. "What does it matter? We're dead already."

Tetra glared at him. "We are not dead. In a few hours we'll be in Federation territory and we'll be safe. Don't borrow trouble."

"What she said," Gaius interjected, wiping the sweat from his brow.

"Are you okay, Gaius?" Pliny asked.

"Never better. Heart's racing, brain is on overload and I'm barely qualified to fly, much less operate a cruise ship alone. This is not a good day for me, thank you for asking."

Pliny put up his hands. "Perhaps a drink or some food will make you feel better?"

"I could go for a fresh tapped ale from Aurora's."

Tetra got up from her seat. "I'll go see what kind of food we have. We shouldn't stress out on an empty stomach."

"I'll be in the observation deck, working on our scriptures," Pliny said, leaving his post. He could feel Aelia's eyes on his back, questions left unanswered.

It was time for him to step up and be a leader.

Chapter 34

Aelia walked into the observation lounge, apple and a tall glass of wine in hand. She found Pliny in his usual spot, with his arm projector turned on and several holographic displays floating above him. He was gesticulating, rapidly moving his fingers and eyes from one location to another. She watched him for a moment, absorbing the fact that his actions were probably their salvation.

As she strode over to him, she could see the intent look on his face through the holograms. She waved the hand with the apple in it. "I thought you should have some food and wine. Nothing's as horrible as writing a deep religious treatise on an empty stomach," she said.

Pliny smiled and plucked the apple from her hand. "You are most kind," he said.

"Doubtful. How is the work coming?"

"Well enough. Not sure if I have enough commandments or whatever, but I sure do have a lot of moralizing and philosophizing. It's just a rework of the book you suggested that I write." He took a bite from the apple.

"Really?"

"Yes, but I have to ask you one thing."

"What's that?" she asked, sitting down next to him.

"Did you tell me to write that book to incriminate myself?"

She hung her head. "Yes. My mission was to collect information about you and expose you and your friends as a cult."

"What changed? Why did you switch sides like that?"

She sighed and took his hand. "Can I be honest with you?" she asked.

"Always. Never be scared to tell the truth. It's one of the most important commandments."

"I've tortured confessions out of dozens of people. Some of them died screaming and pleading their innocence at *my hands*. I can't do that anymore. I can't serve a nation that inflicts pain on its helpless citizens, and deludes itself into worshiping long-dead gods." She paused, dabbing a tear from her eye. "Breaking away from the Pantheon was the hardest thing I've ever done. They had me from birth and were grooming me for greatness. But, once I heard of the singularity, I knew that the world is more beautiful and freer than our religion would have us believe. Almighty gods should have nothing to fear from mortal minds. That's my speech. Your assignment was different—you're nothing like any of the heretics the Imperial Pantheon preaches against."

"Why, thank you. So you're saying you had a change of heart?"

"In so many words, yes."

"You're not telling me the whole truth," he said.

She hung her head and her cheeks heated. "I love you, Pliny Augur. You're the first man to pay attention to me, that's true, but you're someone special and I will fight for you, even if there is no place for me by your side."

Pliny leaned back, stopping mid-chew. He swallowed, wiping his mouth with the back of his hand. "Wow," he said. "I didn't think you liked me that much."

"You think I'd destroy my career and promotion for just anyone?"

"Fair enough. What are we going to do about it?"

She reached over and grabbed his free hand, passing him the wine glass. "Have a drink and let me help you with your book. We can worry about the rest later."

Pliny patted her thigh as he took a sip from the wine glass, before holding it to her lips. She took a sip, her mouth enjoying the dryness of the wine, and the reminder of a home she'd never see again.

She leaned in, pressing her lips against his. This was Aelia's second kiss, and her heart raced. She wanted to do this one right. He pulled back, smiling. "This is going in the book. 'We must seek to become one with each other.' Spiritually speaking, of course. I'm not that kind of Gothi."

"Do it, I like seeing you inspired," she replied "What's a Gothi?"

"Some kind of ancient Terran priest. I came across the term when I was researching connectedness and old human religions," he replied. "I liked the sound of it."

***

Aelia was curled up on the couch next to Pliny, pointing out areas of improvement and inspiration based on her years of fanatical subservience to the Pantheon. It was a fun exercise—she'd never had the ability or occasion to question an idea before, and she found it much more stimulating than torturing another human. She tried not to think of her area of expertise. She couldn't handle the guilt of all the pain she had caused, for nothing. She didn't even know if the Terrans would accept her.

Perhaps she was too far gone to be worth saving. She rubbed her eyes, trying to stay awake. Their ordeal was taking its toll on her, and she was fighting to remain calm and sharp.

Pliny stretched, and she cuddled up. She may be damned by her people, but she had not yet cost him his life, or his soul. She could no longer harm innocents and she would retrain in a viable skill—if she ever got out of this mess. Time would tell.

She pointed at one line. "Can you explain that part?" she asked.

"Oh, it's nothing much. It's just the notion that we're all part of a whole, and we're to take care of each other to the best of our abilities. I call it attraction and connectedness. I think I made up a word there, but nothing else seems to fit."

"So we're all bound together by a force?"

"Exactly. The thing I saw while I was dead must be the singularity. It looked exactly like the black hole from the cruise in x-ray mode. I could feel its realness, its surging tide of all that is sentient. The good, the dark, the light, the pain. It was all there."

"I see. So how do we get there?"

"We live in union with each other. We share, we laugh, we make love. Everything is about coming together, rather than labels that divide." Pliny whisked the line back into place with his hand. "I hope this is good enough," he added.

"It will be," Aelia said. "You can make this happen."

Chapter 35

The ship rocked, sending the shimmering lights of Pliny's holographic display into a momentary chaos. He sat up straight, and shook Aelia awake. "Something's happening?" he asked.

The door to the lounge opened, admitting Felix. "Get your asses in here. Now. Do or die, *Gothi*," he said.

Pliny was on his feet, the ship rocking beneath him. He steadied himself on the back of the couch before stumbling to the door. His holographic images shimmered as they trailed him. There was no time to turn it off. If he was to save his friends, he'd need to think fast.

The bridge smelled of fear. It was oppressive, and everyone's gaze was fixed on the screen. A concerned man looked into their faces, his eyes taking in all and nothing at once. His smirk was a contrast to his blank dead eyes. Pliny swallowed. He'd never seen a Terran before. They were human, as he was, but Terrans themselves were forbidden to visit, land, or live on Roma IV.

The man spoke, and his voice was hollow, as though he was speaking into a tin can. There was a lag between his voice and the sound that came out of the speakers. This must be the fabled translation technology that the Terran Federation possessed. "Greetings, Roma spaceship. How can we be of assistance? I see you are traveling towards our borders quite quickly, with interceptors in hot pursuit."

"I am Gothi Pliny Augur," Pliny began as he was interrupted by a great lurch. The entire ship shook. "We are seeking religious asylum!"

"We do get such requests from time to time. However, not all refugees take a space cruiser for their chosen method of escape."

"It seemed a good idea at the time," Pliny said.

"What is the name and nature of your religion?"

"We are the Children of the Singularity. We are a philosophical religion intent on understanding the flow of humanity and bringing lives together." The hull creaked and groaned as another harpoon attempted to knock them out of the time-drive.

"I see you're in quite a bit of trouble. Run afoul with the Imperial Pantheon, have you? Is that an Executor I see behind you?"

Aelia stepped forward. "I am. Former Executor. I have decided that my life is fulfilled by helping and connecting with others, not suppressing free thought."

"And if I contact the interceptor firing those lances, would I hear a different story?"

"They are the authorities," Pliny said. "We're heretics, plain and simple. We'll be put to the question and sentenced to torture and death if we're handed over to the authorities."

The man paused for a moment, stroking his chin. "I see. Set a course for the coordinates I'm sharing with you. Do not deviate. Terran interceptors will be with you shortly." The screen went blank.

"You got all that, Gaius?" Pliny asked.

"Already on course. We'll be there in about an hour, provided we're still in one piece."

Pliny sighed and sank down into his seat at the edge of the

room. He looked over his comrade's faces. Tetra chatting with Felix, Aelia standing next to Pliny and Gaius paging through documentation desperately looking for a way to get them safely into Federation space. Pliny got up and walked over to Gaius, who sat straight up in his seat. The man was fidgeting.

Pliny placed his hand on the man's shoulder. "Hey, how are you holding up?" he asked.

"I've been better," Gaius replied.

"I'm sure you have. Think we can keep them off our backs?"

"I found a setting that will magnetize our hull and cause the javelins to glance off. It was made for attacks by space pirates." He laughed. "The designers thought of everything."

"Keep at it. I'll buy you a bottle of your favorite wine once we're out of here."

"With money from what job? And do the Terrans even know what good wine is?" Felix asked.

"Point taken," Pliny said, sighing. He hadn't considered that he'd be penniless and forced to rethink his career and his life. Would there even be a need for picobot assembly in the Terran Federation?

Felix continued: "Let's hope they have portable translators and a goo factory. At least we can learn the language as we go. I just want to have a life back."

"Don't we all," Tetra cut in.

A dull thud rocked the ship. "What was that?" Pliny asked.

"Just a lance being repelled by our magnetic field. This feature might save us all."

"You're doing a great job. It will all be over soon," Pliny said, before returning to his desk on the far side of the room. Gaius nodded, turning back to his files.

"Do you think they'll manage to board us?" Tetra asked.

"I wouldn't bet on it, but I think the *Mistress* will send us a few more nastygrams before we reach safety. That is, if they actually take us in," Gaius said.

Pliny spoke next. "Let's think of better things. Do Terrans have wine? Pubs? Theater and art? It will be a fresh start—an adventure for us all."

Felix raised a glass of wine. "To wine!"

Pliny raised his hand, as if to ward off the stars whizzing by on the screen. Was their new home somewhere out there? Would the Terrans be as welcoming as reputed? He was deep in thought when the communication system activated, blaring an alert through the silent room. "Who is it?" Pliny asked.

"Both of them, at the same time."

"This should be interesting, put them on."

The screen winked to life, overshadowing the star-lit vista. To the right was Mistress Marcia, and to the left was the mystery man.

"Gothi, good of you to join us," Marcia spoke. "Turn back now and forget this madness. You can find we'll be very merciful."

The man spoke, nearly cutting her off. "I am Alrik Smithson, diplomatic representative of the Terran Federation. I implore you to ignore this woman. She is clearly a power-mad Roma IV despot and cannot be trusted. The Terran Federation welcomes you and your crew with open arms."

Pliny's heart fluttered. Safe. Were they saved? Alrik continued: "I'd prefer seeking the promise of safety from the unknown to returning to an assured death back home. I've been told what you people do to heretics."

Marcia's eyes flashed. "Fool! How would they live in a world that is not their own? They don't speak the language. They don't have a job. These barbarians don't even make proper wine."

Alrik sighed. "I assure you, Gothi Pliny, we do make excellent wine, among other things. We have personal-sized translators. You're not the only planet with its own language, you understand. Meet us and we'll talk."

"I insist on being a part of this discussion. You have no legal grounds to intercede in this case. It is an internal affair," Marcia demanded, her face turning bright red.

"Do you know what I see here?" Alrik asked. "I see the destruction of people who asked the wrong questions, possibly to the wrong people. Is that a crime here? No, it is not. We cannot abide the torture and killing of innocent free thinkers."

"How dare you decide what is and is not permitted in the Empire, Smithson."

Pliny raised his hand and walked toward the screen. "We shall not yield to you, Mistress. Go back to your ebony desk and spend your days as you wish, but leave us out of it. I formally declare that we will not return to the Empire. Instead, we shall join with, and serve, the Federation as contributing members of society, as our philosophy demands."

"Juno strike you down, how dare you assume what is good for our society?"

Alrik laughed. "So it's settled. Five of our interceptors are en route. I suggest you turn back now, before a full-scale war breaks out over a handful of mere *heretics*. It's your decision, *Mistress*. Always a pleasure."

"Fine. You win this battle, Alrik, but not the war. It is our destiny to eradicate the Terran Federation. As for you heretics— leave Roma space and never return. Only death awaits you here." Her side of the screen went blank.

"Congratulations on your impending Terra Federation citizenship. I look forward to meeting you all personally. For now, hold your course and we'll see to it that your nemesis does not cross our border. We'll have you integrated with us in no time."

Pliny smiled. "Thank you, sir, and blessings upon you and the Federation." It seemed an occasion for blessings, so he threw it

in to keep up with appearances. If he were to be a Gothi, he must
act like one.

The *Void Star* dropped out of hyperspeed around a cluster of small asteroids. Pliny squinted into the emptiness of space, trying to see an interceptor, a planet, anything. They were back in real-time, and they were vulnerable to weapons fire and boarding. Aelia stood next to him. He reached out and took her hand. She was shaking, so he tightened his grip, hoping to provide reassurance. He wasn't sure which of them was truly the leader. She'd lead them to the *Void Star* and helped them escape, but he'd been the connecting force between all of these very different people. Could it be that humans in and of themselves were attractors, acting in the same way as a singularity? He'd have to explore that thought at a later time.

The lead interceptor broke off from the others, gently approaching their ship's battered and scorched hull. Lines of gray and white were burned into the black hull. "Let's get to the docking port," Pliny said. "Get out of this monstrosity and never look back."

The others fell in line behind him. The mood was solemn, not even Felix commented on the inevitable. They kept their heads down as they walked along the dimly lit corridor and hoped the Roma forces would not launch a stealth attack. When they reached the airlock, Gaius walked up to the control panel and pressed a few buttons before stepping back into line. The circular gear-shaped doors creaked open, and Pliny winced, trying to minimize his obvious discomfort.

A tall man stepped through the portal. It was Alrik. A wired plug protruded from his left ear and he was grinning. "Greetings, unaffiliated humans." His lips did not match the sounds they heard. Was this a kind of telepathic technology they'd never heard of? "Welcome to the Terran Federation."

Pliny walked up and extended his right hand. Alrik took it and they shook. Pliny was impressed at the man's height—he was at least a hand taller than Pliny, if not more. "We thank you for your generosity and kindness. May we all be good citizens to your fair Federation."

"I'm sure you will be. As for the rest of you, state your name and last position held."

"Aelia Vellus, Executor of the Imperial Pantheon."

"Tetra, philosophy student."

"Felix, picobot assembler."

"Gaius, pilot in training."

Alrik nodded. "I would think that this voyage would give you your wings. You all have bright futures in the Federation. Even philosophy for its own sake is a viable career path, and you may philosophize about anything you wish. Though, Aelia Vellus, we would like to debrief you, an Executor is quite a prize you see, so few defect, understandably."

Aelia nodded. "Of course. I must atone for my prior actions by exposing the Pantheon however I can."

"So that's it? We're saved?" Pliny asked.

"Not quite. We need to fit you for translator modules and retrain and integrate you into our society, but compared to what you've been through, it's trivial. Come, join me on my ship. Leave this hulk for my men to study. We have much to discuss."

"Indeed we do," Pliny said. "Indeed we do." He took Aelia's hand and ducked through the portal to a new life. Towards hope.

The End

Thea Gregory is a science fiction and fantasy author. When she's not crafting her multiverses, she enjoys daydreaming, gardening, and many kinds of video games. Her creative process is often accompanied by her mischievous cat, Bonk, who occasionally disrupts her flow. She resides in the Montreal area with her partner and, of course, Bonk.

Did you enjoy *Worshipers of the Black Hole*? Please consider helping me out by leaving an honest review.

Sign up for my monthly newsletter and receive a free short story set in the *Worshipers of the Black Hole*'s universe. Want to see what becomes of Pliny's vision? Download *Singular Truth*:

https://planetthea.com/free-story/

For more of my work, including the mathematical sci-fi horror novella *n-Space*, the *Zombie Bedtime Stories*, and *The ABACUS Protocol* series, join my newsletter or follow my social media:

Website: https://planetthea.com
Threads: @author.thea.g
Instagram: @author.thea.g
Facebook group:
https://www.facebook.com/groups/TheaGregory
https://www.facebook.com/TheaIsisGregory/

www.ingramcontent.com/pod-product-compliance
Lightning Source LLC
Chambersburg PA
CBHW031306120726
47906CB00003B/919